The V
A DI Eri
Boc
N

The Wordsmith
A DI Erica Swift Thriller
Book Thirteen
Copyright © 2024 M K Farrar
Edited by Emmy Ellis
Cover Design by Marissa Farrar
Published by Warwick House Press

License Notes

Publisher's Note

Content Advisory

I know it's not common to see these kinds of things in crime books, but I felt this story needed one. The content advisory does contain spoilers for the book, however, so I have placed them on my website rather than writing them here. If you would like to see them, you can find them at www.mkfarrar.com

Chapter One

She stumbled off the East London night bus, clutching the strap of her tiny bag across her shoulder. The heel of her shoe caught in a drain, and she almost went flying, except a pair of hands caught her.

"Get away from me."

She shook the man off, not wanting him to touch her.

"Aww, come on, Chelsea. Don't be like that."

She spun to face him. "Like what? Pissed off that I saw you giving your Snap to some skanky bitch? How the hell do you expect me to be?"

They'd only been dating three months. This was supposed to be their honeymoon period, but it seemed James wanted to spend the honeymoon with other girls, too.

He laughed, the bastard. "She asked! What was I supposed to say?"

She sensed the gazes of the other passengers, their faces pressed against the window to catch what remained of the argument. She and James had been fighting the entire journey, hissing at each other in that way people did when they were angry but didn't want anyone else to overhear. It had been clear everyone had been listening, though. A couple of drunk lads kept yelling their opinions from the back, and a creepy man in his forties, sitting across the aisle from her, had been staring at her bare legs in her short dress.

"How about 'no thanks, I've got a girlfriend, and she's standing over there'?" she suggested.

3

They weren't the only people to get off the bus. Several others did, too, and Chelsea and James moved out of the way to let them pass. The creepy man got off, and she shuddered as his gaze raked down her body again, lingering on her legs. She tugged down the hem of her black dress, but there was only so far it could go.

The man shoved his hands in his pockets and kept going, his head down. She was glad he'd put distance between them.

James reached a hand out for her again. "It's not like we ever said we were exclusive."

Her jaw dropped, and she yanked her hand out of reach. "I didn't think it *needed* to be said. We've been living in each other's pockets for the last three months. You said you loved me."

He gave a sheepish shrug. "Yeah, well, it was what you wanted to hear."

She glared at him. "You are such a fucking prick. If you think you're still coming back to mine, you can think again."

It was his turn for his jaw to drop. "Seriously? That means I have to get right back across the city. It's almost two in the morning."

Chelsea took perverse delight in the thought of him either having to spend another hour on a night bus to take him back in the opposite direction, or else spend a fortune on a black cab. Served him right for trying to play her. Who the hell did he think he was?

She was trying her best to act with bravado, but deep down, her heart was breaking. She'd actually thought she'd met someone she'd connected with—a relationship that might last longer than just a few months—but she'd been wrong. James was no different to any of the other men she'd met. The moment someone new had batted her fake eyelashes his way, he couldn't help himself.

She put her hands on her hips. "That sounds like a *you* problem."

"Fuck you, Chelsea. You're such a bitch. I didn't even do anything."

She tutted her tongue against the roof of her mouth. "I don't need to listen to this shit."

"Chelsea, babe, you're overreacting."

"Leave me alone, James. I mean it. I don't want to see or hear from you again."

Chelsea spun on her heels and marched away from him.

Her rented house, which she shared with two other girls, was about a ten-minute walk from where the bus had dropped her off on Mile End Road. It was late, but she'd walked this way a million times before.

His voice chased her down the street as she stormed off, still staggering slightly in her heels. She'd had a few drinks, and while she wasn't completely wasted, she knew she'd feel like shit in the morning. She'd feel even worse now she and James had broken up.

A sob hitched in her chest, and she gulped it down. She tried to blink back tears, and the East London street blurred. The place was grubby, in a way it so often was at this time of night. Discarded takeaway packets, still clogged with soggy chips and pieces of kebab, intermingled with half-crushed beer cans and cigarette butts. The bare metal bones of some market stalls hunkered down at the kerb. In only a couple of hours, the area would come back to life. Stallholders would arrive with vans filled with produce, and street cleaners would make the place sanitary again.

A stupid little part of her—the part that still believed she loved him and that they could have had a future—wanted James to come running after her and tell her that he'd made a terrible mistake. But then she remembered how he'd laughed at her and forced herself to harden her heart.

That son of a bitch, how dare he?

She turned off the high street, slipping onto the quieter roads of the housing estate. Most of the homes on either side of the road were in darkness at this time of night, though one or two windows were still lit up. It comforted her to know she wasn't the only one still up. What were those people's reasons for still being awake? Were they also nursing heartbreak?

A tear slipped down her cheek, and she batted it away with the ball of her hand. That prick didn't deserve her tears.

She became aware of other footsteps on the pavement. What direction had they come from? It was hard to tell—the acoustics were strange at this time of night. Chelsea glanced over her shoulder but couldn't see anyone. It was dark, the shadows hiding secrets.

The farther she got from the high street, the more isolated she felt. It wasn't as though she was completely secluded. There were buildings all around her, but that also meant there were plenty of darkened doorways and side alleys. All perfect places for someone to leap out and grab her and drag her back in to rape and murder her.

An unsettling thought occurred to her.

Had the creepy man followed her off the bus?

She didn't think so. He'd gone in the opposite direction. But maybe he knew a cut-through and had doubled back and got ahead of her. He'd overheard her and James fighting on the bus, and so maybe had guessed that she'd walk off and would be alone and vulnerable.

She reached into her handbag for her phone, wondering if James was still on the high street, waiting for a return bus. She could call him and ask him to come back to her flat after all. Though having the phone in her hand made her feel as though she was only giving someone another excuse to attack her—this time for her expensive iPhone—she swiped the screen for James' number and then pressed the call button. She had the phone on speaker, hoping the sound of a male voice might intimidate whoever was around, but instead of James' voice, the call went straight to an automated answer machine.

"Shit," she hissed.

Had he put his phone on 'do not disturb'? Or was it only her calls he wasn't answering? His way of punishing her for not letting him come back.

In the air, she caught the familiar scent of cigarette smoke. A pang of longing swept over her. She'd quit a couple of years ago, but every time she smelled someone smoking a cigarette, it reminded her of that first one of the day with her morning coffee, and it made her want to start up all over again. She could do with a cigarette right now.

The footsteps filled the air again, and she spun around, determined to locate the cause.

The street behind her was empty.

Her heart beat faster, her breath catching.

Maybe she should go back the way she'd come? No, that was stupid. She only lived around the corner. She'd have to come back this way to get home. She considered calling one of the girls she lived with, but she was also aware of the time and didn't want to bother them if she was just freaking herself out. It wasn't as though they were particularly close; she'd found the house share advertised on the university Facebook page.

Chelsea stuffed her phone back into her handbag and kept going. The footsteps had vanished, and there didn't appear to be anyone else around. She must have been imagining things.

She rounded the corner, heading into her street. On the other side of the road, were railings that divided the residential street from the small industrial area beyond. She didn't know what went on there, only that there were a number of large metal storage containers, like the kinds that are used to transport things on ships.

A man stood directly in front of her, his back to the railings.

Chelsea drew up short, a yelp of shock escaping her lips. It was him—the man from the bus. It must be. But, as her initial shock faded, even in the dark—the street lamps barely doing enough to illuminate more than the spotlights directly beneath them—she could tell this wasn't the same man. This one was younger, with a completely different build.

Then something else occurred to her. He didn't seem to be standing straight. He was at a kind of odd angle—not slumped—but not quite upright either. Her heart jolted, pumping adrenaline through her veins.

Her gaze travelled down his body.

His feet weren't touching the ground.

Chelsea staggered away, back in the direction she'd come, wanting to create as wide a berth as possible. She stumbled off the pavement and ended up in the middle of the road. She wanted to get past him, to run away, to make it home and hide beneath her bedcovers. Her position brought her parallel to his body, and she clamped her hand to her mouth.

At the back of his head, the metal railings pierced the soft part where his neck met his skull, skewering him onto the sharp black point.

Chelsea opened her mouth and screamed.

Chapter Two

It was still dark, the moon a white bite mark in the otherwise black sky.

The crime scene had already been set up. Police tape blocked off the junction in three directions, and floodlights had been brought in to illuminate the spot where the victim had been found. Response vehicles were parked on either side of the road. A white privacy tent had been erected to prevent nosey people getting a look or photograph of the body.

DI Erica Swift placed her hand across her belly. She was only four months along, and already she felt like a whale. She'd have no choice but to end up behind a desk at this rate. She wasn't going to be much good to anyone then.

Her partner, DS Shawn Turner, was in court that morning, testifying about a prior case, which was why he hadn't attended the crime scene with her. She'd left him still sleeping, a part of her hating him a little for not having to haul himself out of a warm bed to step out into the night.

The road where the body of the young man had been found was just off Mile End Road. It was a busy area. It would be light soon enough, and then people would start getting up for work or school, and then the mayhem would begin. Violence wasn't exactly unusual around here, but a man's body hanging on a railing would definitely get some attention.

She hoped they'd be able to take him down before then.

Crime scene photographers moved carefully around the area, snapping pictures of the body in situ. Like her, they were dressed head to toe in white protective outerwear.

Erica snapped on her gloves, signed in with the officer protecting the scene, and ducked beneath the cordon.

She approached the police sergeant in charge of the scene, Sergeant Diana Reynolds. The sergeant's short blonde hair was hidden beneath the white hood, and a pair of glasses framed her blue eyes.

Sergeant Reynolds spotted her approaching. "DI Swift. Thanks for coming. Sorry about the early hours."

"Can't be helped. Criminals tend not to stick to nine-to-five."

She gave a small laugh. "Very true."

"So, what have we got?"

Sergeant Reynolds turned towards the victim. "White male, mid-twenties approximately, found dead shortly after two a.m. by a pedestrian."

"Any ID?"

Reynolds shook her head. "Nothing in his pockets. We'll search the local vicinity in case he dropped his wallet or phone. We might get lucky. He's been printed at the scene, but nothing on file for that either, so it doesn't look as though he has a record at all."

"Just an innocent passerby then," Erica mused.

"Perhaps, or someone who got himself caught up in something he shouldn't."

Finding the identity of the victim would go a long way to helping them with their enquiries. They'd be able to trace his final steps, who he'd been with, track down credit card usage and get mobile phone records. But until they had his name, they didn't have much at all.

Someone would be missing him. Perhaps not right now, but certainly in the next twenty-four hours or so. He wouldn't show up for work, or a partner might notice that he hadn't come home when he was supposed to. There were very few people who could vanish without it worrying someone.

The reporters would be buzzing around soon, too. A description of the man would be released, and someone might recognise him from that. She was confident they'd find out the identity of the victim, it was just a matter of when.

Erica took a few steps around the body, using her torch to get a better look at the victim. The floodlights that had been brought in helped, but they still created points of shadows that could hide something important.

The man appeared to be suspended on one of the railing heads, which was in the shape of a spear, the puncture wound at the soft part beneath his skull. The metal was slick with dark blood, and there was more blood on the pavement below.

Erica pointed at the railing. "Any indication that this *isn't* the cause of death?"

Reynolds shrugged. "Currently unsure. I don't think he'd been dead long when the witness found him. There's no sign of rigor mortis setting in, and the body was still warm to the touch. I'd say we're looking at him being killed no longer than a couple of hours ago."

It was still warm for September, one of those Indian summers. Another month or so, and the temperature would have dropped enough that the body would have cooled rapidly.

"The volume of blood also suggests that he was killed here," Reynolds ended.

"Any other injuries on the body?"

Reynold's grimaced. "Yes, one in particular. You need to see."

The man wore a shirt that had once been white but was now stained red with blood. With a gloved hand, Sergeant Reynolds edged open the front of the shirt. The buttons were missing, scattered across the ground beneath them. Several deep cuts ran from the victim's clavicle, down to his pectoral muscle, and back up again.

Erica shone her torch on the wounds. She counted three, with the middle one at an angle.

"What are they from?" she wondered out loud. "They look deliberate."

"That was my thinking, too."

Erica twisted her lips. "Did someone torture him before they killed him? I'd say this rules out a fight that went wrong, then."

"Or they got in a fight, and whoever won decided to leave their mark on his body."

Mark. That word resonated with Erica. Was it a symbol of some kind? Had they seen this before? Was it some kind of message? A gangland thing?

"Let's make sure we get some close-up photographs of the wound, best we can. We'll know more after the post-mortem. What about signs of a struggle?"

"Nothing obvious. There are no contusions or bruising on the victim's face to signal there's been a fight. The backs of his knuckles aren't scraped or bruised either. No signs of ligature marks around his wrists and ankles, or signs of strangling."

"He's not a big man, but for someone to have impaled him on this railing it would have taken some serious strength."

Erica glanced up, wondering if he could have been dropped from a height from something suspended—a piece of building equipment, perhaps—but there was only the night sky above her.

"Or it was more than one person," the sergeant suggested.

Erica turned her attention to the small industrial area on the other side of the railings. A number of shipping containers were positioned at various intervals, but she couldn't see any signage indicating what they were used for.

"What kind of business is that?" she asked.

"Storage for dropshipping, as far as we can tell."

Erica frowned. "Dropshipping?"

"Yeah, you know, like when people order stuff online from social media ads. They store goods in these containers?"

Erica nodded in understanding. "Let's find out if they've got any security cameras. They might have caught something. What other cameras do we have around here?"

Reynold's jerked her chin in the direction of the high street. "There's an ANPR camera on Mile End Road."

This was a built-up area. There were bound to be more.

"We're going to need to go door to door, see if anyone either saw anything, or has security cameras or a doorbell camera." She glanced at all the vehicles parked down the street. "Let's match each of the cars to their owners, too. Make sure nothing is out of place."

From the amount of blood on the pavement beneath the man's feet, it seemed to her that he'd been killed right here. She tried to visualise the moment—two men struggling, only for one to lift the other high enough to impale him on the spike of the railing. Had it been done deliberately, or had it been an accident, and upon realising the other man was dead, the killer had fled the scene?

Erica turned her thoughts to the witness. "You said the body was discovered by a passerby?"

"That's right. A young woman called Chelsea Booth." Sergeant Reynolds checked her notebook. "She's twenty-three years old and a student at Queen Mary's University, studying English Literature."

Erica felt sorry for today's students. That they would finish their degree saddled with the sort of debt they'd probably never pay off was shameful to the system. Most would just end up in regular jobs anyway—the kind of jobs they'd probably have got if they'd just gone straight into work at eighteen. She understood if a person wanted to become a doctor or a solicitor, or something similar, but many of these people with arts degrees simply ended up stuck with a lifetime of debt before their lives had even properly got started.

Reynolds continued, "She was on her way home after a night out with her boyfriend. She got off the night bus on the high street and found the body only a matter of minutes later. I don't think she'll be walking home alone again anytime soon. She lives around the bend. She's pretty shaken up, understandably."

"I bet she's wishing she took an earlier bus."

"Yes, she'll be regretting her decisions. She placed the nine-nine-nine call at two-thirteen this morning. The operator struggled to understand what she was saying at first, she was so distraught. It took a little while to get her location and what had happened out of her. Luckily, we had a response team not far away, so they were able to get to her within a few minutes."

"Where's the witness now?"

"One of my officers is sitting with her at home. She was extremely upset and since she lives so close, it made sense to let her sit somewhere comfortable."

Chapter Three

It wasn't hard to find the address of the witness. Not only was it right around the bend, on the same street the man had been killed, a police car was parked on the road directly outside.

The place looked much the same as any of the other houses on the road. They were all terraced, with tiny front gardens and a faint air of neglect. This wasn't a wealthy area. It was full of student and social housing.

Erica paused outside the house. Her shirt and jacket were baggy enough to hide her stomach, but she still found herself pulling her jacket shut. She was definitely at that stage where she looked more like she'd eaten a large dinner, and people would never comment on it in case they were wrong. That was fine by her. The last thing she needed was for people to treat her any differently. Why was it women were seen to be something fragile when they were pregnant, rather than admiring them for working and keeping a family together, at the same time as creating a whole other person?

She pressed her finger to the bell, and it sounded somewhere deeper inside the house.

A young male uniformed officer answered the door.

She showed him her ID.

"DI Swift," she introduced herself. "I was hoping to speak to the witness."

He shuffled backwards to let her in. "She's through here."

The stairs were directly in front of her, and a narrow hallway led past them into the living room. To her left was a small galley kitchen which contained two other young women. Chelsea lived with housemates, who were also students, and Erica assumed this was them, woken by all the commotion. Erica would get members of her team to interview the housemates, too. They might have seen or heard something that would be useful.

Erica followed the officer into the living room to where Chelsea Booth sat perched on the edge of her sofa, her hands clamped between her knees. She was a pretty woman in her early twenties. Her short dress rode up her thighs, and her mascara was streaked down her face. Pale tear marks ran through her foundation.

"Miss Booth?" Erica smiled kindly at the young woman. "I'm DI Swift, the Senior Investigating Officer on the case. I realise it's been a long night for you, but I wondered if I could ask you some questions?"

Chelsea was completely pale and still shaking, though not from the cold. Her eyes were bloodshot from crying, and dark shadows created the illusion of bruises beneath them. Of course, it was late—although it could also be considered early now, depending on your point of view—and the witness hadn't slept at all.

She lifted her wide blue gaze to Erica's. "If you think it will help. I did already talk to one of the police officers, though."

"Mind if I sit?" Erica gestured to a chair opposite.

"No."

The furniture had that worn, mismatched appearance of items that had been found mostly at charity shops. A couple of framed photographs of more young women, all around the same age, and some mostly burned-down candles, sat on the mantelpiece.

Erica sat. "We'll need to take an official statement from you, too, but not right now. Get some rest first and then come down to the station and give it."

"Do you know who he is yet?" Chelsea asked. "The victim, I mean."

She gave a brief shake of her head. "We're still working on it. Any information you can give us may help us narrow things down."

"I don't know what more I can tell you. I only found him." Her voice caught. "I wish I hadn't."

"Coming across something like that can be very traumatic, and we'll make sure we put in some support for you, but I'm afraid I do need you to go over it again."

"I'll do whatever I can to help. It's horrible to think something like that has happened right around the corner." She shuddered. "What if the killer is still out there? What if he saw me and knows where I live?"

"I'm sure the person responsible is long gone," Erica reassured her. "He wouldn't stick around with so many police swarming the place."

That wasn't completely true. It wasn't unusual for killers to hang around to witness the discovery of their work. They got off on the shock and distress the killing caused for whoever found them. There were plenty of cases where it was later proven that the killer had watched the fallout of their actions in a gathering crowd. They liked to pat themselves on the back about how clever they were to be able to stand so close to both the police, who they considered stupid, and their victim. It was one of the reasons the police always checked the photographs of the crowds that inevitably gathered around a crime scene. The perpetrator of the crime could sometimes be picked out among the faces.

"What time did you get off the bus?"

"Just after two a.m. At a guess, I'd say about five past two. I was out with my boyfriend, James."

"Had anything strange happened on the bus?"

"Nothing more than normal. The night bus always contains a dodgy group of people." She seemed to think of something. "There was this one man. He kept staring at me. He gave me the creeps. He got off the bus at the same time we did. At one point, I thought he might be following me."

"Are you able to describe him?"

"In his forties, I think. Dark hair, though it was slightly receding. He was a little overweight, and maybe five-ten. Not particularly tall."

It couldn't have been him who'd been responsible for the murder. If he'd been on the bus with Chelsea, there wouldn't have been time for him to find his victim and kill him and get away. But there was a possibility he had seen something—a person running away from the crime scene, for example. He could be a potential witness, as could any of the people who'd exited the bus with Chelsea.

They'd be able to get security footage from the bus and see who'd got off at the same time.

"You said you were out with your boyfriend?"

Chelsea sniffed and wiped her nose. "Yeah, well, I'm not sure he's my boyfriend anymore. We had a fight."

"I'm sorry to hear that. Did he get off the bus with you?"

She squeezed her hands between her knees and didn't look up. "Yes, but I told him he wasn't coming home with me and that he needed to get back on the bus and go home. I wish I hadn't now. I wish I hadn't been alone when I found that man."

"It must have been very distressing for you. We're going to need to speak to your boyfriend. There's a possibility he saw something that might help. What did you say his name was? James?"

"James Moore. I can give you his phone number."

"That would be helpful."

Chelsea picked up her phone from where it lay beside her on the sofa and swiped the screen. Her hands were still shaking.

"It's lucky I didn't delete his number," she said with a tight smile, holding the device out to Erica so she could take down the number.

Erica took the phone and jotted it down. She had no idea if the boyfriend would have seen anything or not, but it was always worth asking. Had he been the one to follow Chelsea home, perhaps wanting to make sure she got back safely, despite their argument? If that was the case, why hadn't he checked if she was okay after she'd discovered the body? Or had he been so shocked at the discovery that he'd turned and run?

If it hadn't been the boyfriend following Chelsea, who had it been?

"I smelled cigarette smoke," Chelsea suddenly announced. "I remembered smelling it in the air, right before I found him."

"But you don't know where it was coming from?"

"No, sorry."

It could have just been someone in one of the nearby houses with a window open, having a sneaky cigarette when they weren't supposed to smoke inside.

"Thank you. That could be useful." Erica made a note for them to watch out for cigarette butts. If it was the perpetrator smoking, then something like that would be easy enough to get a DNA sample from.

"Did you see or hear anything suspicious before you found the body? Maybe someone running away?"

"Only that I thought someone was following me, like I already said. I heard footsteps but when I turned around, no one was there."

Someone must have heard something. You didn't impale a man on a railing post without there first being some kind of a struggle. In this area, if someone had heard sounds of a scuffle, they'd have probably dismissed it as just another fight after the pubs kicked out. But maybe, if they learned there was more to it, they'd reassess.

"Okay, thank you for your time." Erica got to her feet. "I'm going to let you get some rest now. If you could give a formal statement tomorrow, I'd appreciate it."

"Of course."

Erica walked past the kitchen and stuck her head in. "Look after her, okay?" she told the two other students. "She could probably use your support."

The two young women were like deer in the headlights.

"Yeah, sure," one said.

The other nodded. "Of course."

Erica let herself out of the property. The sky was already lightening to a murky blue-grey. She glanced at her watch. It was approaching six a.m.. She was going to need a strong coffee, she thought, and then checked herself. She wasn't supposed to be drinking coffee because of the baby. A cup of tea would have to do, but she could already feel herself sulking about it. Because of her age, she was technically a 'geriatric pregnancy', a term that Erica thought should be forever scrubbed from the English language, so she was considered a high-risk pregnancy. She'd generally felt well enough, though, the odd bit of morning sickness in the early weeks, but that was all.

It was going to be a long day, and an even longer one if she wasn't allowed a decent hit of caffeine.

Chapter Four

Frances Gilchrist stood at her kitchen counter, a mug of coffee in front of her. In one hand was a slice of toast that she was eating while standing up. In the other she held her phone, mindlessly scrolling through Facebook.

She was trying to take her mind off the worrying mole she'd discovered on the back of her thigh this morning. It had been itching, and she'd scratched, thinking she'd just been bitten by a bug. When she'd taken out a mirror to look at it, she'd noticed it was a mole, and now it was raised and scabby and bleeding. While she had never been one to use sunbeds—with her fear of cancer, she'd never do that—she'd done her fair share of sunbathing in her younger years.

Now the mole was like a burrowing insect in her mind, squirming through her flesh to lay its cancerous eggs inside her. She pictured the eggs whisking through her bloodstream, depositing themselves in her lymph nodes and internal organs, taking root and growing.

Just the thought filled her with utter terror.

She lifted her gaze from her phone to where her husband, Matt, sat at the kitchen table, shovelling spoonfuls of cereal into his mouth. He had a tea towel tucked into the opening of his shirt, just below his Adam's apple. He hadn't yet put on his tie. Good thing, too. It would have probably ended up in his cereal bowl.

Frances couldn't stand the stuff. Even seeing him eating it turned her stomach. Sloppy goop. He dribbled milk from the corner of his mouth and then wiped it away with the back of his hand.

Should she tell him about the mole? She wanted to, but she already knew what he'd say—that she was overreacting, and it was nothing, and she'd just caught it with her nail while she was scratching.

He'd say it was no different to the headache she'd convinced herself was a brain tumour the week before, or the heart palpations she'd had the week before that had surely been a heart attack, or the blurry eyesight that had made her think she was going blind before that.

No matter how far back she went, there was always some crisis or another. It was hardly surprising he was dismissive of them now.

With her job as an author, it was important that she have an overactive imagination, but there were definitely times when she wished it wasn't quite so active. It didn't matter how much she tried to convince herself that whatever was worrying her was nothing, she could never push it completely from her mind. At some point, one of her fears would come true, and what if it was that symptom that she told herself was nothing?

Trying to distract herself via Facebook, she paused on a news article from a local page. Crime was her thing, so she clicked on it and started to read. Her pulse picked up its pace, and she felt a little strange, as though she'd suddenly realised she was asleep.

"Have you seen this?" she asked her husband,

He glanced up from his breakfast. "Seen what?"

"The police found a body off Mile End Road last night. A man."

He gave a snort of disgust. "Place is getting rougher with every passing year."

"Maybe, but that's not what I'm talking about. The man was found hung on the railings that wrap around a park. Speared on them by the back of his head."

Matt screwed up his nose. "Do you really have to share those kinds of details right when I'm eating? That's grim."

He'd never paid much attention to her books. He was more than happy about her writing when the royalty cheques came in, but he'd never bothered to actually pick one up and read it. He said he just didn't like reading fiction, and she guessed that was fair enough, but it still stung a little than he'd never really tried. Or maybe he had, and had hated it, but didn't want to tell her.

"It's just that..." She trailed off, feeling stupid. It didn't mean anything, did it? It was just a coincidence.

"It's just what?" He sounded impatient.

"I wrote an almost identical scene in one of my books."

He laughed. "Are you saying someone was inspired by what you wrote and decided to recreate it for real?"

She hadn't been saying that, but now he'd spoken the words out loud, it jangled through her nerves, alarming her. That hadn't happened, had it? It was just a coincidence. It had to be.

He must have caught her expression. "Frances, seriously, that's not what you're thinking, is it?"

"No, no," she said hurriedly. "Of course not." Then she hesitated. "Do you think I should speak to the police?"

He stared at her like she'd lost her mind. "About a scene you wrote in a book?"

"It's not just a scene." She didn't like his dismissive attitude. "The whole book is based around that one murder, and it's described in exactly the same way as I just read about. Even the victim matches the description of my victim in the book."

He shook his head. "What? Young white male? I mean, that could be anyone."

Frances glanced back down at her phone and nodded. "Yeah, sure. I know that."

Why was this bugging her so much? Of course it wasn't connected to her book. It wasn't even as though that many people had read it. It wasn't like she was one of her author friends who were getting Netflix deals and huge advances. She considered herself lucky that she was able to pay her bills by writing her books and didn't need to have a day job. That was more important to her than all of the other stuff. She had her fans, too, but so far none of them had been creepy or inappropriate. Most were women over the age of fifty who'd never treated her with anything other than respect.

She gave a small laugh and tried to shrug it off. "Forget I said anything."

Matt always acted as though her work was little more than a hobby. He was the one with the big important job in the city, the one who wore the suit, and was taken out for flashy dinners, and often had to go away to cities like Paris and New York and even Sydney on business. She just pottered away in her office, talking with her imaginary characters. She was fully aware that the neighbours probably thought she was just a housewife, being kept at home by her incredibly successful husband. And she was grateful to him for what he'd achieved. If it wasn't for the amount of money he brought in, maybe she'd have had to work an office job and she'd never have found the time to really get her foot in the door of publishing.

He got to his feet and plucked his suit jacket off the back of the chair. He slipped it on and then walked over to her and planted a kiss on the top of her head.

"See you later."

"Aren't you going to wish me luck?"

He paused. "What for?"

"I've got that signing in Dulwich today. Remember?" She checked the time. Actually, she needed to get going herself if she wasn't going to be late.

"Oh, yes. I'm sure you'll get a few people turning up."

Her stomach dropped at his dismissiveness. "Hopefully, it'll be more than just a few." The publishers had been marketing the signing for the past month. It would be so embarrassing if she showed up and there were only a handful of seats filled. She wasn't a fan of these things, but she knew she had to make the effort if the publisher was going to re-sign her for more books.

She'd only recently handed her last completed manuscript over to her editor, a book with the working title of *Seize the Dead*. She hated this part, the fear of what he'd say about her latest offering. A part of her was always terrified that her editor would turn around and tell her it was terrible and they couldn't possibly work on it. She believed she had a reasonably thick skin and could handle the occasional bad review from a reader, but if her publisher dropped her, she didn't know what she'd do.

Chapter Five

Erica was back in the office. It was still incredibly early, and she'd had time to get the incident room ready for when the rest of the team came in.

She called a briefing to bring everyone up to speed and make sure they all knew their actions for the day.

She was losing one of her prized members of the team. DC Hannah Rudd had passed her sergeant's exam and was being transferred to a new C.I.D.. Erica would miss her input, and their team was definitely feeling a little high on testosterone. She would have preferred to have some more women around. Their new member was twenty-three-year-old Detective Constable Lewis Crowe. He seemed impossibly young to Erica. Had she really reached that age where everyone seemed younger than her? How had that happened so fast? She needed to treat him as an equal but instead she found herself wanting to send him home to his mum and protecting him from all the bad shit he might come across in day-to-day life in this job.

On the board behind her, she had pinned photographs of the victim, together with a map of the area, plus pictures of the business that backed onto the railings. There were close-ups of the man's injuries, including the cuts on his chest, though they were hard to make out with so much blood on his skin and clothes.

Erica paused at the photographs, studying them for a moment. Why had the victim been cut? Had it been an attack? She tried to picture the killer with a knife, slashing out at the victim. Had it been to keep the victim away? Except he'd caught him on the chest?

But the victim's shirt hadn't been cut. So had the cuts been done post-mortem? And if so, why?

Movement came from behind her, and she turned to see members of the team filing in. A couple of greetings of 'morning' reached her ears.

She gave them all time to find their seats and get settled before she began.

"Right, let's get on with this, shall we? I appreciate that it's early." She took in all the bleary eyes and coffee in reusable mugs clutched in hands. "Before I start, can everyone welcome Detective Constable Lewis Crowe to the team."

Everyone shifted in their seats to smile at the new arrival. Lewis lifted his hand in a half wave.

She nodded at one of her older members. "Jon, if you could give him the tour once we've finished the briefing, I'd appreciate it."

DC Jon Howard nodded. "Sure thing, boss."

"We're also going to be saying goodbye to Hannah in a couple of weeks, since she's leaving us for greener pastures."

Good-natured booing went around the room, and Hannah covered her face with her hands and laughed.

Erica continued, "I'm sure you've all heard by now that the body of a young man was discovered shortly after two a.m." She ran through what they'd learnt so far. "Finding out the victim's identity is of utmost importance. Without it, we're going to struggle to understand what preceded the murder. Did he know his killer? Was this a wrong place at the wrong time situation? It was shortly after two in the morning when the body was discovered. Where had the victim been before he arrived at this point? Or had he been on his way somewhere? Is he local?" She paused to take a swig of her decaff coffee and did her best not to grimace. "I need someone to work with MisPer, see if they've got anyone who matches our John Doe. Also, keep your ear to the ground for any new missing persons reports that come in. He's well dressed. I don't think he's homeless or a vagrant, so chances are someone is missing him."

"I'm happy to take charge of that, boss," Hannah said.

"Thanks. I need someone going through CCTV around the area, see if we caught anything unusual. We also need to get the CCTV footage from the night bus that the witness was on. We know both her and her boyfriend got off, but so did several other people, including a currently unidentified man in his forties." She looked to the new arrival. "Lewis, think you can manage that?"

"Absolutely."

"I've got uniformed officers going door to door around the area. Someone might have heard something. Where the murder occurred, there are four different directions the killer could have gone in. Over the top of the railings, and into the business behind, down the street where the witness lives, back down the road, or else towards Mile End Road, where he—or perhaps she—would have passed our witness.

"The victim's feet weren't touching the ground"—she indicated one of the close-up photographs, where the man's toes weren't quite skirting the pool of blood beneath him—"so he must have been lifted which requires a good amount of strength which means the killer is most likely male. The victim most likely weighs around seventy kilos, and if there was also a struggle, such a feat wouldn't have been easy."

Murmurs went around the room.

"The victim had three lines cut into his chest." She pointed at the photographs again, this time of the shirt. They hadn't yet got any information from the pathologist, so the images were a bloodied mess and not very clear. She hoped they'd be able to update them soon. "They look too deliberate to have been made during a fight. I don't think they're from someone lashing out with a knife and cutting someone as none of the clothing was nicked. We have a search team covering the area, but as of this morning, no weapon has been located. The amount of blood lost from the wounds suggests the victim was still alive when he was cut. What does it mean? Have we seen it before anywhere? Is it a gangland sign? I'm going to need someone to check into previous cases to find out."

"I can, boss," Jon offered.

"Thanks. Remember, it's not necessarily murder cases we need to look at. Check previous GBH cases, too. You might need to go back a few years. Start with five initially."

He tipped his fingers to his forehead in a salute.

"Let's think about how the suspect would have got to and from the scene of the crime. Would they have had blood on them?" She couldn't imagine they'd have been able to avoid it. Perhaps they were wearing black so it was less visible, plus it had been dark. "Would he have just walked off down the street like nothing had happened? Was he on foot or did he have a vehicle? If there was a vehicle, blood would have been transferred from the suspect's clothes and skin to the interior. We've got all the cars parked in that area at the time of the murder being examined, but something tells me they'd be long gone."

Erica turned back to the map and indicated the area behind the railings. "Why did the suspect choose that spot to conduct the murder? Was it just that this particular corner isn't overlooked where the rest of the street is? There's a business located directly behind where the body was found. Let's find out a bit more about it. All we know right now is that it's to do with dropshipping. But who owns it? Who works there? Are there cameras? Have the employees been aware of any recent disturbances? Even without the name of the victim, we have plenty we can follow up on, and I'm sure we'll find out the victim's identity very soon."

Erica made sure everyone had their actions and then dismissed the meeting. They had journalists to deal with as well. A violent murder like this was always going to attract attention. It had already been reported on, but the journalists would be hounding them for updates.

As she headed back to her desk, already thinking about what she could eat next, her boss's office door opened, and his head poked out.

He caught her eye. "You got a minute?"

"Sure."

Thinking mournfully of the biscuits in her desk drawer that were going to have to wait a little longer, she slipped into his office.

DCI Gibb's gestured to the chair on the opposite side of his desk, and she sat heavily.

"Sounds like you've got a violent case on your hands. I just wanted to make sure you're okay to work on this case in your condition."

He would be retiring soon. Perhaps she'd have even considered taking on the job, if it wasn't for the pregnancy. Her daughter was getting older now, and, in a couple of years, would be making her own way to and from school, and probably spending more time with friends. She wouldn't need Erica in the same way she had when she'd been little, though it had always been a struggle on Erica's part—the sense of constantly being pulled in two directions and failing at both. Now she was going to have to do it all over again, right at a time when she should have been coming out of it. She'd always told herself she didn't want the job, that there would be too much time spent behind a desk, but now she knew she couldn't take it, it suddenly seemed more appealing.

"I'm pregnant, sir, not sick. I'll be fine."

"You've done your work health and safety?"

"Yes, sir, of course. I understand that you're covering your back, and the back of the force, but no one is forcing me to be here. I don't want anyone to treat me any differently."

"I understand." He paused and then said, "Erica?"

"Yes."

"I'm only making a fuss because we care about you."

She cracked a smile. "Thanks, sir. I know."

Chapter Six

She left Gibbs' office and returned to her desk for her much-needed biscuits. At the moment, she was either starving hungry or nauseated; there didn't seem to be any in-between.

As she munched on them, trying not to get crumbs in her keyboard, she went back over the case file for any details she might have missed. It hadn't helped that it had still been dark when she'd been there. Even with the floodlights that had been erected, it wasn't the same as seeing a place during daylight hours.

She wondered how the witness was doing. Hopefully, the young woman had managed to get some rest, but Erica doubted she'd ever be able to walk past that particular spot without reliving the moment of finding the man's body all over again.

She went through each of the photographs again. The heads of the railing were like spears, or they would never have been sharp enough to pierce the back of the victim's neck, penetrating his cerebellum, like it had. Why did the business behind the railings feel the need to have such dangerous spikes? They weren't tall—easy enough to climb over if it wasn't for the points. What were they defending against? She was surprised no one local had complained about them, but then maybe they had.

That pulled up a question: had the suspect already known how sharp the railings were? If so, he'd been there before and scoped the place out.

But why had the victim been there, too?

Movement came from the other side of the office, and she looked up to spot Shawn's familiar figure.

He headed straight over.

"How was court?" she asked him.

He grimaced. "Dull as hell, just like always. So much waiting around for five minutes on the stand."

"Think the guy will do time?"

"Most likely. The whole thing was caught on CCTV. I was only there to give my testimony on his frame of mind at the time of the arrest. The defence is trying to argue that he had temporary insanity and didn't know what he was doing when he attacked her."

Erica shook her head. "This is the one who was stalking his ex-girlfriend, right? Didn't he send her threatening messages for months before he tried to shove her in the back of his van?"

"Yeah, that's the one. Like he was insane all that time, too. I'm sure he'll go down for it, just don't know how long. That poor girl is probably only going to have a couple of years of peace before he's released again." He flashed her a smile. "Anyway, enough of all that. How are you feeling?"

"I'm fine, focused on this new case." She brought him up to speed on the events of the day.

He raised an eyebrow. "Sounds like you've had a far more interesting day than me. What do you need me to do?"

"Can you coalesce with Sergeant Reynolds, find out if their door-to-door has come up with anything yet?"

"No problem." He eyed the new body at the desk. "How's the new kid doing?"

She shrugged one shoulder. "Good, so far, though it's early days."

"He's been dropped in the deep end with this one. He'll get those training wheels off soon enough. Any leads?"

"Not yet. We need to find out who the victim is."

He lowered his tone. "And how are *you* feeling? You must be tired after such an early start and, well...you know." His gaze dropped to her stomach.

They hadn't made the pregnancy common knowledge yet. Obviously Gibbs knew, but that was all. She didn't know how much longer she could keep it a secret, but she didn't want anyone treating her differently.

She still wasn't one hundred percent sure how she felt about it all. The thought of going back to the newborn stage, waking up multiple times a night, and dragging herself through each day exhausted, didn't exactly fill her with joy. She still remembered how isolated she'd felt when Poppy had been a newborn, and how out of her depth she'd been. She liked to think of herself as a capable woman, but in those early days she'd been anything but. Poppy was finally of an age where she was a little more independent, and, instead of appreciating that new independence, Erica felt like she'd ended up right back where she'd started.

Shawn, of course, was over the moon about the whole thing. He fussed around her to a point where she was snappy and irritable, and then just plagued with guilt for being a complete cow to him. None of this was his fault—well, it was in part, but she didn't want to blame him for it. She just wished she could embrace the whole idea in the same way he could, but it didn't affect him the same way it did her.

Poppy had only recently started at the local high school. It had seemed like a big transition to Erica, but her daughter had taken the whole thing in her stride. She'd been more than ready for it, and it helped that her cousins had already been at the school, and that most of her primary school classmates fell into that catchment area, too. That didn't stop Erica being nervous about it. Officers went into the high schools to give lectures to the kids about the seriousness of knife crime, but there was still a rise in knife crime in schools. Metal detectors and wands could be used to check anyone entering the grounds, but that it had come to schools being treated like airports filled Erica with both fear and sadness. Though it was mainly teenage boys who were the victims of knife crime, Erica didn't want Poppy to have to go through the trauma of being exposed to that kind of violence either.

She pulled her thoughts away from her personal life to refocus on the case.

"We should go back to the crime scene after lunch," she said. "I'd like to get a better look at the business the railings back onto, speak to whoever owns it."

Shawn threw her a smile. "You're the boss."

Chapter Seven

Frances Gilchrist sat at the signing table, behind a stack of books with her name on them, and tried not to feel nervous. She hated doing these things, though both her agent and her publisher said that it was more necessary than ever that her readers were able to connect with her. In these days of social media, people liked to feel like they had access to you twenty-four-seven. Every text message, every DM, every email was supposed to be read and responded to in a matter of minutes. Any longer, and people took it as a personal snub.

Her agent, William Hart, stopped and put a hand on her shoulder to give it a reassuring squeeze.

"You look like you're about to throw up," he said.

"Thanks. That's not a compliment."

"You're white as a ghost. Maybe a little blusher would help."

"Christ," she muttered but bent down to her handbag for her compact and the lip and cheek tint she carried with her. "You know I hate doing these things."

William was about a decade older than her and had been in the book business pretty much since he'd left Oxford—something he was always keen to remind her of. He came from old money and also liked to remind her how the agency had been his father's, and when he'd completed his degree in English Literature, where he'd got first class honours, it had been obvious that he'd needed to pick up the ropes.

He had two kids, both boys, and his wife, who was also at least a decade younger than William, spent most of her time either running round after the family or having lunch and Pilates sessions at the golf club near Chelmsford where they lived.

Though Frances was the talent he got a cut from, he somehow had a way of making her feel like she was the poorer cousin.

"They're here to see you," he reassured her. "They're your fans. You have nothing to be nervous about."

She straightened, holding the tub of tint in one hand and the open compact with the mirror in the other.

"Have you met the fans lately?" she said as she dabbed some on her cheeks and lips. "Some of them can be brutal, and they have no hesitation in saying exactly what they think. Someone posting about *Dying Days* in a big crime Facebook group the other day saying that they thought the characters were poorly drawn out and the twist was obvious and about two hundred other people jumped in to agree with them."

He pursed his lips at her in disapproval. "I've told you not to read those posts."

"You've also told me I have to interact with the readers more, and it's a bit hard to ignore them when they just pop up on my feed when I'm casually scrolling."

He shrugged. "Keyboard warriors. They'd never say it to your face, and anyway, none of those people will be here today. These are your real fans. They love your books, or they wouldn't come all this way to meet you."

Dying Days was book six in her crime series set in London, and though it was her most recent release, she'd actually written it over a year ago. She hoped no one was going to ask her questions about any specific ins and outs of the story, because there was a good chance she'd have forgotten. She'd already finished book seven, and her editor, Blaire Foster, said he was nearly done working on it.

"Are you ready, Ms Gilchrist?" Melissa, the independent shop owner asked. "It's time to open the doors."

Frances put the tint and mirror away and forced a smile that felt more like a grimace. "As I'll ever be."

She was doing a reading from the book first, and then she'd take questions, and finally sell some paperbacks and sign some copies for readers, too.

Ninety percent of her readership were women, and most of them were above the age of fifty. At only thirty-two herself, she always felt as though she'd be judged for being too young to write a decent story, having not had that much experience herself. She knew it was just her own imposter syndrome coming into play. It wasn't as though her books had hit multiple bestseller lists, but they sold well enough that she could pay her bills and her publisher kept signing her up for more.

The store's owner opened the doors, and the readers piled in, many talking animatedly to each other while they were finding their seats. It was an audience of mostly women, as expected, but there were a few men dotted around as well. Frances suspected they were partners or husbands dragged along as company rather than her actual readers.

She gave them enough time to get seated, and for any late stragglers to arrive, and then glanced over to William who gave her the nod.

It was time to start.

Melissa joined Frances and spoke first, introducing her to the small crowd. A smattering of applause filled the space as the owner stepped away and allowed Frances to take the room.

She stood and rounded the signing table so she wouldn't have a physical barrier between her and the readers. Her book was in hand, a pink tab marking out the place where she'd be reading from.

Frances hoped her voice didn't tremble too much as she read from a chapter of her book, a particularly gory scene where her serial killer tortured one of his victims. When people looked at her, she knew they'd never expect the sort of gruesome, violent crimes that formed themselves in her brain and came out via her fingers on a keyboard. She was only five feet two, and the bobbed blonde hair and blue eyes said more primary school teacher than crime writer.

Frances managed to get through the reading, though she could feel her cheeks burning. Was her heart beating too fast? Was it a warning sign? She forced herself to take some slow breaths and smile at the audience. Everything was fine. She was safe. She didn't want to make a fool of herself.

"Thank you so much, everyone. I've got a little time to take some questions and then I'll sign some books for you."

She felt presumptuous even thinking that someone would want her to sign books. She still felt like a nobody, a nothing. Why had these people even come to see her? They probably just didn't have anything better to do—it didn't mean they were actual fans.

Frances took questions. They were all the usual ones: where do you get your inspiration, do you ever base your characters on people you know, how long does it take to write a book?

A man hung out at the back. His head was down as he browsed the bookshelves. This was supposed to be a ticket-only event, and regular customers weren't meant to be in here. They'd checked tickets on the door. Maybe he worked here?

The questions were over, and she took a quick break to grab a drink before settling herself behind the signing table. The attendees began to form a line, ready to get their books signed.

Frances felt her gaze being drawn back to the man who was still at the rear of the shop.

She felt as though he was watching her, but every time she looked over, he had turned his face, or even his back. Was she just being paranoid? It was bothering her enough that she was struggling to focus. When someone told her what their name was, it didn't go into her brain at all, and even when she asked them to repeat it, she still didn't hear properly. In the end, she had to get them to write it down.

"I adore your books," a woman in her mid-fifties gushed. "Every time you release a new one, I go back and read from the start of the series again in preparation."

"That's wonderful to hear," Frances said honestly. "It means a lot to me that you take the time to read my stories."

"Oh, not at all. I absolutely love them."

"Who can I make the book out to?" Frances asked.

"It's Tracey. Tracey with an 'e.'"

Frances scribbled out a personal message and signed her name. She closed the book again and handed it back to Tracey with an 'e'. "I hope you enjoy this one, too."

Nearby, someone coughed, thick and productive, and Frances fought the urge to pull the collar of her shirt up to cover her mouth and nose. After the events of recent years, even something as apparently harmless as a cough or cold now had the potential to be life-threatening. A spike of anxiety went through her. It was another reason why she hated doing these things—the possibility of catching something was sky-high. People wanted photographs and would put their arm around her and stand so close she'd want to scream.

"Oh, I will. I've already read it."

Tracey stepped out of the way and let the person behind take her place.

Another woman approached her table.

"I'm sorry," Frances said, "would you excuse me just for one minute? I'll be right back."

"Of course," the woman replied.

Frances slipped out of her seat and hustled William into the corner so she could speak to him.

She kept her voice low so as not to be overheard. "Who's that bloke? The one at the back?"

William pursed his lips. "Not sure. I'm guessing a reader. Why?"

"He just doesn't seem overly interested in what I have to say."

"You want me to go and tell him to pay more attention?" he teased.

"No, of course not. He just seems out of place, that's all."

"I expect his missus has dragged him along."

"Yeah, you're probably right." She chewed on her lower lip. "He's just distracting me. I'm getting a bad vibe."

There was something about him. An atmosphere. Dark, broody, shifty.

"You've been writing too many crime novels."

She gave a small laugh, to show she agreed with him, but it contained no humour.

Frances saw both storylines and people up to no good everywhere she went. When she spotted a couple of broken number plates lying on the side of the road, she assumed they must have been used on a getaway car. A foreign passport she'd found must belong to someone who'd been trafficked. Perhaps she just had a suspicious nature, but when that was combined with an overactive imagination, it also gave her plenty of storyline fodder.

Her imagination was one of her strongest points, but it could also be her greatest enemy.

Chapter Eight

E rica and Shawn returned to the scene of the crime.

Places always felt different in the daytime. Somewhere that seemed intimidating at night was just a regular street in the day. Of course, this one didn't look so regular. The streams of blue-and-white police tape blocking off the road highlighted it as being the place a crime had been committed. Then there were the police vans and people in white protective clothing.

They were still searching the area for any clues. Something as small as a dropped cigarette butt could be enough to crack a case. Markers had been placed all around the area, but particularly where the body had been found. The pavement was stained dark with blood, and, though it was harder to see against the black paint of the railings, Erica knew blood had dried on the metal, too.

They both pulled on protective gear and approached the scene.

Officers noticed them and nodded their greeting.

Erica stepped back and gave Shawn some space.

This was his first time seeing the scene, and she stayed silent, aware he was taking it in with fresh eyes. He might easily spot something important that she'd missed. He crouched to take in the pool of blood, above which the victim had been found impaled, and then rose again and took a wider view of the vicinity.

"If the perpetrator brought the victim here," he said, "how did they get here? The victim isn't the largest of men, but it still isn't easy to move a full-grown man around. That suggests a vehicle being involved."

She played devil's advocate. "Or, had the victim walked here? Had he been with the person who'd killed him at the time? Did they know each other? Could they even be friends?"

Shawn twisted his lips and nodded. "If it wasn't for the cuts on the victim's chest, I'd consider that this was a fight that got out of hand, but those cuts appeared far too deliberate to be the case."

She tried to picture the moments that led up to the victim being impaled upon the spike. Had the killer brought the victim to this spot deliberately? If so, why? It wasn't overlooked, unlike many of the areas around here, so had it been for a reason as simple as privacy? Knowing he'd be less likely to be seen?

She voiced her questions to Shawn.

"Sounds more to me like they were sending some kind of message," Shawn replied.

She had the same thought herself. "Question is, what?"

Erica liked questions—even ones she didn't yet know the answer to. They opened up avenues of possibilities, and there was always going to be a good chance that one of the questions she asked was going to be the right one.

Her hand went to her stomach, automatically protective, but she caught herself and snatched it away. The last thing she wanted was to draw attention to herself in that way. The fewer people who knew, the better. Erica hated gossip, and this was going to be office gossip of the century. Not only because of her age, but because she was effectively Shawn's boss. She knew she wouldn't be able to hide the pregnancy forever, but she wanted to try for as long as she could. She didn't want to be treated differently either. She was good at her job—respected—and she felt like this would undermine her authority.

"Let's go and check out the business the railings back onto," Shawn said.

The entrance was on an adjacent road. To reach it, they had to leave the crime scene, discarding their outerwear, and go back out onto the main road, and then turn left again.

There were no signs up that indicated what took place on the site. Clearly, the owner didn't expect customers to come on site. Coiled barbed wire sat on top of the chain-link fence that surrounded the front of the property, though Erica assumed it was mostly for show since there was nothing similar at the rear. She counted at least six shipping containers positioned at various intervals. One appeared to have been converted into an office space, and two cheap, plastic chairs sat outside the door.

Signs warning to 'keep out' were also attached to the fencing. She was almost surprised not to see a couple of large dogs on chains barking at them.

"Friendly-looking place," Shawn commented.

"Wonder what the owner is like?"

She glanced up, checking for security cameras. To her relief, two were positioned near the entrance. With any luck, they might have caught something.

Shawn checked his notepad.

"On Companies House, the business is registered to a Mr Luke Heale. He's got a record. Nothing serious, but one charge of fraud, another for moving stolen goods. Looks like he's in the habit of setting up businesses, letting them go bust, and then just setting up a whole new one right after."

"Doesn't sound encouraging. Think he might be doing something dodgy with this one?"

"I think we need to delve into this place a little more closely. Maybe they're connected."

She knew she had a suspicious mind—that was her job—but she couldn't help wonder if someone had been trying to send a message to whoever owned the business. Maybe it was more than just random bits of tat from the internet that was being stored in those containers.

Shawn shrugged. "Probably something we need to consider."

"If he is, he might not be too keen to hand over his CCTV footage."

Erica tried the gate, and it opened. An old Range Rover was parked inside.

Movement came from inside the office, a shape passing across the dirty window, and, a moment later, the door opened. A man appeared, his wide forehead furrowed into folds.

"Mr Heale?" Erica asked.

He was a large man in his early fifties with an almost bald head. The image was completed with some bad tattoos and a dirty white shirt.

"Who's asking?" He sniffed. "You two look like the filth."

She took out her ID to hold up for him. Beside her, Shawn did the same.

"We're detectives, Mr Heale. DI Swift and DS Turner. I'm sure you've heard about the man's body that was discovered on railings at the back of this property in the early hours of the morning."

"Yeah, of course I did. Half my property's been cordoned off. I've got a business to run, and I can't access half my stock."

"I apologise for the inconvenience, but I'm afraid it can't be helped. There's a chance the murderer, or the victim, may have crossed your property, and we can't risk there being any contamination of evidence." She glanced around. "What exactly is it you do here, Mr Heale?"

"Thought you knew that already? Dropshipping."

"Yes, but dropshipping what exactly?"

He shrugged. "Whatever's going to be popular at the moment. When it's approaching Valentine's Day, I do a lot of love heart jewellery, and at Christmas it's pretty lights and baubles for the tree. I watch the market and give it what it wants."

"I'd like to ask you some questions," she said. "Was there anyone on the property overnight?"

"Nope. I was at home. The place was empty."

"Mind if we take a look around?" Shawn asked.

His small grey eyes narrowed. "Why? You think the killer might be hiding in one of my containers?"

Shawn shrugged. "Stranger things have happened."

"Do you have a problem with us looking, Mr Heale?" Erica put her hands on her hips. "We can always get a warrant, if you'd prefer?"

He hesitated, as though considering his options, and then shook his head and turned to go back inside. "I'll just get the keys."

He reappeared a moment later, a bunch of keys in one meaty hand. "Which one do you want to check?"

"All of them," Erica replied.

He jerked his chin at the closest container. "We can start here. Don't know what you think you're going to find, though. I keep these things locked up tight. Last thing I want is to get robbed myself."

He stopped in front of the container, jangled the keys and the lock, and then lifted a metal pole to open the door.

"Here you go," he announced.

The container was filled with cardboard boxes upon boxes. It was impossible to even step inside. They reached from floor to ceiling. There was no possibility that someone could have sneaked in here, even if they'd managed to get past the bolt on the door, which was highly unlikely.

"Thank you for your cooperation, Mr Heale. It's appreciated. Have you had any trouble around here recently?" she asked.

"Other than what happened last night, nothing that stands out. There's always going to be problems with teenagers hanging around, wanting a place to smoke weed, or drink. Sometimes they vandalise things. I've had the occasional homeless person creeping around, trying to find shelter for the night, but they don't cause too much trouble."

"Have you had any problems with anyone? Personally, I mean? Or perhaps professionally."

"Why do you ask that?"

"A body was left on your property, Mr Heale."

He scoffed. "Not my property. That fencing belongs to the council. This site just backs onto it, that's all."

Erica shared a glance with Shawn. They needed to check that. Shawn gave a tiny nod to show her he had already made a note of it. The killer most likely wouldn't know that detail.

"Can I show you a photograph of the victim? So far, he's unidentified. I wondered if you might recognise him?"

She pulled up a picture of the man's face.

He leaned in and frowned. "No, I don't think so. Sorry."

"That's okay. I appreciate you taking a look. You said no one was on the property overnight, so what time did you leave here yesterday?"

He seemed to consider this. "Six-thirty, I think. Maybe a little after that."

"And the property was all locked up after you left?"

He nodded slowly. "As far as I'm aware. It's generally not a good thing to leave anything unlocked around these parts. People here would nick their own gran if they thought they could get away with it."

"Who else works here with you? You can't manage all those boxes alone, surely?"

He scuffed one foot along the ground, glancing away. "I've got two people who help with packing, but that's all. I pretty much run this place single-handed."

"Are they around?"

"No, I told them not to come in 'cause I can't access half the goods anyway. Figured there was no point in paying them to sit around."

"I'm going to need their names and addresses," she said. "They might have seen someone suspicious hanging around recently."

He seemed uncomfortable, shifting his feet from side to side, and cleared his throat. "I'm paying them cash in hand. I haven't exactly done due diligence about whether they're allowed to work."

"What are you saying? You think they might be here illegally?"

So he was probably paying some desperate people a pittance to pack orders for him.

"I wouldn't say that. I mean, they're foreign workers. I just haven't checked their visas yet, that's all. It's on my to-do list."

"I'm still going to need their names and addresses. I'm not interested in who you do or don't hire, Mr. Heale. The only thing I'm after is the person who killed that man."

She had to remind herself that Luke Heale wasn't under investigation here.

"I can give you their names, but like I said, I don't have their addresses."

"You have their phone numbers, though. You must do if you told them not to come in today. I'll need those from you, together with their names."

He exhaled a breath and scratched at his forehead. "Fine." He fished his phone from his pocket. "I've got them on here."

He read out the names and numbers, and Shawn took out his notepad and pen to jot them down.

Would these people even speak to the police? From past experience, Erica knew they were more likely to either run away or clam up if they thought the cops wanted something to do with them. There was nothing to stop Mr Heale warning them that the police wanted to speak to them either.

Erica indicated the security cameras. "I noticed you have cameras here. Any chance they're working?"

He gave a small snort of laughter. "Around this area? Of course they are. I pay for online storage so I can watch back over anything that might have happened."

That was good news.

"Are you able to send me the footage from last night? The cameras might have caught something."

He gave a brisk nod. "Yeah, I can do that."

She hadn't expected him to be quite so amenable. "That would be great, thanks." She handed him one of her cards. "My email is on there."

"When do you need it?"

"Soon as you can."

He shrugged. "Okay, I'll see what I can do."

"Thank you for your time, Mr Heale. We'll be in touch if there's anything else."

Together, they left.

"What do you make of him?" Shawn asked.

"I think he's telling the truth. He doesn't know anything about the murder that took place last night. But do I think he's shifty as hell?" Erica nodded. "Yeah, I do."

Chapter Nine

As they returned to the car, Erica's phone rang.
She checked the screen. It was the number for the mortuary. She answered, hoping it would be Dr Lucy Kim, but instead it was the male and far more sedate tone of Dr John Hamilton that greeted her.

"DI Swift," he said, "I'm nowhere near done with the post-mortem, but I cleaned up the body, and I think you need to take a closer look at something."

She had the phone on speaker and glanced over at Shawn, who nodded.

"We can be there in thirty minutes," she said.

"Great. See you soon."

"Sounds like he found something," Erica said. "Hopefully, it'll help us track down the victim's identity."

They drove through East London, arrived at the mortuary, and found a spot to park.

Natasha would be picking Poppy up from school today. It was impossible for either of them to get away early enough to pick her up when they were in the middle of a big case like this. Poppy was getting older now, and Erica was conscious that it wouldn't be long before Poppy was able to walk home by herself and be in the house alone. She didn't want Poppy to turn into a latchkey kid.

Then she remembered that she was going to be home soon, with a new baby. Everything was going to change. Perhaps she needed to be grateful that she was being given that time, both with Poppy and the new baby. She knew Poppy was going to be delighted to have her mum home, and to be a big sister, too.

"Ready?" Shawn asked her.

She'd been sitting there, lost in thought. "Yes, sorry. Let's do this."

"You're pale." Shawn's lips pinched. "Here, eat one of these."

From his pocket he produced a small three-pack of ginger biscuits.

She raised an eyebrow. "You're carrying those around with you?"

"Emergency biscuits," he said with a grin.

She needed to eat regularly now, something this career didn't always work well with. If she left it more than a couple of hours, she started feeling nauseated. Being around dead bodies while already feeling like she was going to throw up was never a good thing.

"Thanks. When this is over, I am never going to eat a ginger biscuit again in my life."

When she was done, she took a swig of water from her bottle and brushed down the front of her shirt. She climbed out of the car, and together they headed inside and signed in at reception.

She'd lost count of the number of times she'd been in this building, but she was always glad she didn't spend all day here. She'd never been a fan of hospitals, and, while this wasn't one, it gave off the same vibe. The smell lingering on the air was similar—cleaning product mixed with illness and death.

Outside of the examination room, they paused to pull on protective outerwear, and then they joined the pathologist.

John Hamilton was a tall, angular man, with a serious personality. He fitted his profession perfectly. Erica imagined that during dinner parties, when people asked what he did for a living, they wouldn't be surprised by the answer.

He offered them both a curt nod. "DI Swift, DS Turner, thanks for coming so quickly."

"We were already out and about," Erica said. "You said there's something you think we should see."

"That's right. Come on through."

They pushed open the door and entered the stark examination room. Unforgiving white light reflected off stainless steel, and a familiar odour of chemicals and death filled the air. Erica did her best to breathe through her mouth and ignored the way her stomach turned.

Hamilton led them over to where a body lay on a slab, covered with a sheet.

"I'm sure you can appreciate that I'm nowhere near finished," he began. "I've taken scans and examined the skin for evidence or unusual markings, but that's all. I haven't started the internal examinations. I wanted you to see this before I open him up."

He reached out to the sheet and pulled it down, exposing the victim's torso.

Right away, Erica knew what he was referring to.

"The cuts on the victim's chest look like more than just cuts to me," he said. "Tell me what you think."

Now the wounds had been cleaned, and they weren't partially obscured by the victim's clothing, they were far easier to see. Standing where she was, at the victim's shoulder, she couldn't quite see what he meant, but Shawn was at the other end of the table.

"It's an 'N'," Shawn said. "The cuts make a capital 'N'."

The pathologist nodded. "That was my thinking, too."

Erica moved her position so she was standing next to her partner. He was right. While the cuts didn't quite meet up to create the letter, they definitely looked like the letter N. Or maybe even a sideways Z.

It was no wonder Hamilton wanted to get them in before he started the full post-mortem. The upside-down, Y-shaped cut he'd have needed to make would have run straight through the cuts already present on the man's chest.

"I've taken photographs," Hamilton said. "Measured and recorded the size and shape of the wounds, too. I believe they were done by a very sharp blade. Possibly even a scalpel."

"A medical instrument?" Erica perked up with interest.

"Yes, but anyone can get hold of them these days. All they'd need to do is order online."

"What does it stand for?" Erica wondered out loud. "Is it the victim's initial or that of the murderer? Or could it be something else entirely?"

Shawn took a couple of steps around the body to bring himself closer to the man's head. "Until we find out the identity of the victim, we're not going to know the answer to the first part of your suggestions anyway."

Erica thought again. "A gangland marking then? I don't recognise it as being a tag of any kind."

Shawn shook his head. "No, neither do I."

Hamilton moved on. "There are a few signs of bruising and abrasions on his arms and wrists, though they're not easy to spot initially because of the victim's tattoos. Do you see here, and here?" He pointed out the marks.

"Do they look like finger marks to you?" Erica asked the expert.

"I'd say so. They're new, too, so would have happened shortly before he was killed—most likely in a scuffle that happened preceding it, but we can't say that for sure. He may have been in a fight with someone else and then come across his killer. I've scraped his nails for DNA in case he managed to scratch his attacker."

"What other identifying features does he have? Anything we can use to ID him?"

"As you can see, he's got a few tattoos. Unfortunately, it seems like half the population under the age of thirty have almost identical tattoos, but someone might recognise them. From the scans I did, he also had a couple of older broken bones." Hamilton went to pick up the printouts from the X-rays. "You can see here a healed fracture of his tibia. I'd say it's a good ten years old. He also broke two fingers, which were also healed. These injuries could easily have happened from accidents, or something as simple as playing a sport. They're not related to your case, but it might help you narrow down his identity."

"Anything might help," Erica said.

"No leads?" he enquired.

"Not yet, but someone will be missing him. I'm sure it won't take us long to find out who he is."

The victim had been well dressed, with a fashionable hairstyle, plus good teeth. This wasn't some vagrant who'd been happened upon by the wrong person.

"Oh, there was one other thing," he said, turning to the back of the room. He returned with a metal kidney dish containing an item. "He was wearing a watch. There's an engraving on the back."

She used a gloved hand to turn it over. *Love Mum X*

"A birthday present, perhaps, or maybe a graduation gift. The watch itself isn't anything too expensive—perhaps worth a hundred pounds—but whoever bought it obviously thought it was nice enough to have engraved. Working-class family, most likely."

Her thoughts went to this young man's mother, assuming she was still alive. Would she be the person who would notice him missing first? It was often the women in people's lives—the wife, the mother, the sister—who reported missing people. Unless, of course, *they* were the missing people. She didn't look forward to the moment when she had to tell this man's loved ones about how he'd been killed. A young life cut short. Life was so fucking unfair.

"Someone might recognise the watch if we do a public appeal," Shawn said. "I don't think he's going to remain a John Doe for too long, though."

Hamilton agreed. "I'll be back in touch after I've completed the post-mortem. I'll test for drugs and blood alcohol levels, of course, and should be able to tell you what he had as a final meal as well. As for the cause of death, it's probably sensible to assume it was down to the large spike embedded in the back of his neck, until we learn otherwise."

Chapter Ten

Before they returned to the office, they stopped for something to eat and drink. Erica needed a more substantial lunch than some ginger biscuits.

Hannah stopped Erica the moment she walked into the office. She hadn't even made it to her desk. She could tell from Hannah's expression that she had big news.

"Boss, I got a hit from MisPer. The victim's mother has reported him missing, and then she saw the news saying a body matching his description had been found." She showed Erica a photograph. "Look like the same bloke to you?"

Shawn had been right about him not remaining a John Doe for long.

"Yeah, that's him. What do we know?"

"His name is Taylor Quigley. Twenty-two years old. Local police have already been to see his mother to confirm his identity. He was still living at home. His mum got worried when he hadn't returned from a night out and wasn't answering his phone. She called around all the friends that she had the contacts for, and they said he'd left the pub to head home shortly before midnight."

"Except he didn't make it," Erica filled in.

"That's right."

"What's his mother's name?"

"Paula Quigley. She's forty-eight. Divorced from Taylor's dad, who doesn't seem to be on the scene much."

"Have either of them got records?"

"Nope. Both clean."

"Do we know which pub he was at?"

"The Masons Arms on the Mile End Road. His mother has given us the names and numbers of the people she thought he might have been with. I've got DC Crowe calling round them all now, seeing what other information we can gather."

Erica considered something. "If his name is Taylor Quigley, I guess that means the N wasn't his initial then."

Hannah frowned. "The N?"

"Yeah, the pathologist has cleaned up the wound, and the cuts on the victim's chest make up either the letter N or possibly a Z."

"So that's not the victim's initial, no. Perhaps that of whoever killed him?" Hannah suggested.

Erica grimaced. "Not the smartest thing to do, carve part of your name into your victim. It would give us something to link them."

"I guess they'd argue it's just a coincidence."

"Or maybe they believe they're smarter than us and won't get caught."

Erica raised her voice to address the room.

"Your attention please, everyone," she called to her team. "We have an ID on the victim. I want everyone finding out everything we can about Taylor Quigley. Let's request his bank and credit card records, find out where he used them last, and also his phone records. Where's the last place we got a ping on his phone? He didn't have his phone or wallet on him when his body was found, so what happened to them? Did the killer take them as mementos or toss them somewhere so it would be harder for us to ID him? Or did he simply leave them somewhere else before he happened upon the killer?" She paused to take a breath. "We're going to need CCTV from the pub's premises, and also any on the street around there. Let's try and narrow down his final proof of life. Did the killer stalk him from the pub? Was he even in the pub with him? We're going to need to interview the friends who Taylor was with, too. Did he mention to his friends that he was going somewhere next?"

Finding out the identity of the victim immediately opened up a whole treasure chest of investigative lines.

"What about social media? Did he have a presence online? Did he post anything before he was killed?" She thought for a moment. "Let's also find out if he has any links with the dropshipping business where his body was found."

"That's still bothering you?" Shawn asked.

"Yeah, there's something about it that seems shady. I don't like the owner. I could be completely wrong, but I'm still wondering if the body was left as some kind of message."

She didn't want to get distracted by it, but she also believed her instincts were to be trusted, and right now they were telling her that the owner of the dropshipping business was up to no good.

She turned to Hannah. "Where does his mother live?"

"Bethnal Green. So he wouldn't have walked that way to get home from the pub. He must have had a reason for going that way, though."

"Or maybe he didn't go that way," Shawn suggested. "He could have been picked up in a different location and transported to the place he died."

Erica pinched her lips. "What time did you say he'd left pub?"

Hannah looked between them. "A bit before midnight, but that's not confirmed yet."

She considered this. "If he left before midnight, and his body was found shortly after two a.m., then that leaves around two hours that he's unaccounted for. Hopefully his friends and the CCTV will help us piece together what he did and where he went. I'd like to speak to his mother." She glanced over to Shawn. "Fancy a drive?"

Chapter Eleven

The Quigleys' house was a two up, two down, terraced, ex-council house. It was small but tidy, with red-brick walls and white, uPVC windows. A low wall ran across the front of the tiny space between the front door and the pavement beyond. They weren't pretty properties, but the owner had clearly tried to do their best with what they had.

A uniformed police officer was already there, having informed the mother of her son's death, and the car was parked on the road outside.

Erica stopped her vehicle behind the police car, and she and Shawn climbed out. They went to the front door, and Erica rang the bell.

Footsteps came from inside, and a female officer in her forties answered it.

Erica and Shawn both held up their ID.

"DI Swift," Erica said, "I'm the SIO on the case. I was hoping to speak with the victim's mother."

"I'm the family liaison officer, PC Clare Stern. Come on in. Mrs Quigley is through here."

They followed PC Stern through the house to a small living room at the rear. Photographs of Taylor were on every wall, and framed and propped up on most surfaces, too. Right from when he was a baby, to some that must have been taken within the last couple of years.

Erica's heart clenched with pain for his poor mother, and she couldn't help thinking about Poppy and the new baby growing inside her. No one expected to outlive their child. To spend all those years giving everything you had to raise them to adulthood, only for some son of a bitch to steal their life within a matter of hours was the cruellest thing to put a parent through. Life could be so damned unfair.

"Mrs Quigley," Erica said, "I'm so sorry for your loss. My name is DI Swift, and I'm the detective in charge of your son's case. I wanted to meet you in person and reassure you that we're doing everything we can to bring your son's killer to justice."

The other woman didn't respond. She just cried with her hands covering her face.

PC Stern sat beside Mrs Quigley on the sofa and spoke softly. "These detectives are here to speak to you. They want to find Taylor's killer."

The boy's mother finally lifted her head.

Paula Quigley was only forty-eight, but in that moment seemed a decade older. Her eyes were dark circles, her hair a frizzy mess, the roots a grey halo, and lines ran deep beside her mouth.

"It was only him and me," Paula sobbed. "His father left when he was just a baby, didn't want anything to do with him, and I raised him by myself. I worried about him so much, but I never thought something so terrible would happen to him."

Erica perched on an occasional chair opposite. "Why did you worry about him? Was there anything in particular that you want to tell me about? Did he get into trouble?"

He had a clean record, so Erica couldn't imagine it had been anything too serious.

Paula shook her head. "No, he was a good boy. I just worried, as a mother. You do, don't you? Growing up in this part of London, worrying he'd fall in with the wrong crowd. Who would do this to him? My heart is broken. What's the point in carrying on?"

"I'm so sorry." Erica reached out across the space between them and placed her hand over the top of the other woman's. "Do you have any other family? Someone we can call?"

She was going to need support. Their family liaison officer could only do so much.

"I have a sister, but she lives in Birmingham."

"Have you told her what's happened?"

Paula shook her head. "I couldn't face it."

"If you have her number, I'm sure PC Stern here can call her for you. Tell her what's happened and that you need her here."

She could tell Paula was considering arguing with her, perhaps to tell her that the sister was too busy, or too far away, but then all the fight went out of her, and her shoulders slumped and she nodded.

"Okay," she said quietly. "Okay. Her number is in my phone."

She found the phone and number, sniffing the whole time, and handed it to PC Stern, who got to her feet. "I'll call her."

Erica nodded.

"What can you tell me about Taylor?" Erica asked Paula. "What kind of things did he like?"

"Just normal stuff lads his age like. Football, going out with his mates. Gaming, sometimes." She wiped her nose with a bunched-up tissue.

"Was he working?"

"On and off. He didn't much like being tied down to a job. Maybe I should have made him pay some more bills or something so he had to stick to one, but I didn't want him to move out."

"So he wasn't currently working?" Erica checked.

"No."

"What was his previous role?"

"Night shifts at a garage in Deptford. He hated it." She gave a small, choked laugh.

"Can I get the name of the place, just so we can ask some questions there? Maybe he had a run-in with someone."

"It was on New Cross Road. I don't know the name."

Erica glanced over at Shawn who jotted it down.

"That's okay. We can figure it out. Do you know if he had any fights with anyone recently? Anyone he fell out with?"

She wiped her eyes. "Not that I know of, but then he didn't really tell me any details. He'd just say he had a shit day if I asked him and go up to his room. I can't believe I'll never see him walk through that door again. Oh God. How am I going to survive this?"

She burst into tears.

PC Stern returned to the room.

"Your sister is on her way."

Paula's sister would have lost her nephew, too, Erica realised. Aftershocks of the crime rippling their way through the family.

"I can sit with her until she gets here," the family liaison officer offered.

"Thank you." Erica got to her feet and addressed Paula. "Can we take a look at his room?

She nodded. "It's at the top of the stairs on the left."

Erica offered the woman another sympathetic smile, and she and Shawn left the room. She took the stairs, hating how she was already breathless at the top, and then pushed open the bedroom door. Shawn followed behind.

A double bed with grey sheets was positioned in the centre of the room. Dark-grey curtains hung open. A flatscreen television was hung in the middle of the wall opposite the bed. A pile of laundry—clean and folded, but yet to be put away—sat on the floor next to the chest of drawers.

She pictured his poor mother wondering what to do with the clothes. Was there any point in tucking them safely away in the drawers now?

It only made her more determined to find Taylor's killer.

There was nothing exceptional about the space. It was a typical single young man's room.

"Looks like he vaped," Shawn pointed out.

There were empty vape juice bottles on the chest of drawers, plus an empty 35cl bottle of vodka stuffed down the side of the bed. But he was an adult and could drink and smoke if he liked.

"Check for a phone or wallet," Erica said. "I doubt he left them here, but it's worth a look."

She used her own phone to take pictures of the room so they could refer back to them. She hated to invade a victim's privacy, but if it meant finding the person who'd killed him, she had no choice.

Not that she was expecting to find them here.

"There's a laptop," Shawn said. "Let's check with his mother that it's okay to take it."

They didn't need to, but it was only respectful. Erica couldn't see the mother standing in their way. Like them, Paula wanted her son's killer to be caught, and there might be something on the laptop that could help them.

Chapter Twelve

B y the time they returned to the office with the laptop, it was getting late.

Erica handed the item over to digital forensics. She'd asked Paula Quigley if she had any clue what her son's password might be, but unfortunately she'd had no idea. Erica wasn't surprised about that. She imagined most twenty-two-year-old men wouldn't want their mother to go digging into their private online life.

She filled her team in on what she'd learned.

"We need to check out the garage where Taylor Quigley worked until recently, see if anyone can remember him having a run-in with anyone—customer or colleague. Him leaving probably has nothing to do with why he was murdered, but it's worth checking up on."

The new guy, DC Lewis Crowe, nervously put up his hand to get her attention. "I've been calling around to the people his mother thought he was at the pub with, and I've narrowed it down to a couple of names. He was with Archie Fergusen and Billy Tidwell. I've managed to speak to both of them."

"Excellent work, Detective," Erica said.

The young man flushed right up to his ears.

"Thanks," he muttered and carried on. "The friends from the pub said he'd had his phone but that he doesn't really use a wallet. They all use an app on their phone to pay for things and keep any cards they want inside the case on the phone."

"Okay, that's good to know," she said. "Do we know what kind of phone?"

"An iPhone, so he's most likely using Apple Pay."

She glanced over to Jon. "Do we have phone and bank records back yet? If we can get a ping on where his phone was last used, that could help us narrow down his final movements. Or if his killer took it, we might even get a lead on his location."

"Not yet, but I do have some CCTV from the street and the shops. I've been able to put together a timeline of his movements when he leaves the pub. He stops at a cashpoint and takes out some money."

"What for? Do we know how much?"

"It was only ten pounds. He used it to visit a chicken shop a little farther up the street that is cash only."

Erica raised her eyebrows. "Someone's trying to evade the tax man." That wasn't their problem, though.

"I watched the footage," Jon continued, "and he staggers as he goes down the street. I'd say he seemed pretty drunk, which means he was also vulnerable."

Lewis piped up. "His friends said they'd had a few beers and a couple of shots, too, so it's understandable that he wasn't exactly steady on his feet."

Erica nodded. "I wonder if the person who killed him saw him as someone who was vulnerable. If so, this could be an opportunity thing. It means the perpetrator might not have known the victim beforehand."

"There's something else," Lewis said. "Apparently, Taylor got into a row with someone at the pub. Knocked into a guy at the bar and spilled beer on him. They had words, but it didn't seem to go any further than that."

Erica addressed Jon. "Do we have that on CCTV?"

"Not that I've found so far, but I've got hours to watch yet."

CCTV work involved hours of meticulous viewing.

"Do we know what time that happened?" Erica asked Lewis.

"Later," Lewis said. "Close to closing." He looked around at the rest of the team. "Could the person he'd had a run-in with have followed Taylor? Decided to take his revenge?"

"It's possible. We need to identify him. Might be worth putting a request for information out to the public. If we can get it on CCTV we can release the images from the footage and find out who he is. Or see if he paid by card at the bar and get a name that way."

"There's something else," Shawn said. "I checked my email when we got back, and we've been sent the CCTV footage back from the dropshipping business. Unfortunately, all the cameras are pointed towards the front of the property, so I'm not sure what use it's going to be, but you never know. The murderer might have been walking the streets before they happened upon the victim. Maybe we'll have a stroke of luck and catch him passing the CCTV."

Erica nodded. "Yes, it's not just the time of the murder that we want to consider. They might have been scoping the area before that."

Shawn held up a finger as though to stop her. "There's one problem, though. The footage only shows from six-thirty that evening. The owner says he doesn't have the cameras running when there are people on site."

She frowned. "That's odd. Why would someone bother turning cameras on and off?"

He raised both eyebrows. "Unless there's something he doesn't want to be caught on camera?"

"Unfortunately, we can't prove that." She huffed out a frustrated breath. "He's allowed to switch his own security on and off when he wants to. I guess it makes sense that he doesn't need it running if he's on site."

Even though she'd given Mr Heale's side of the argument, she wasn't totally convinced about that. She hadn't liked the man.

She forced a smile and glanced around her team. "Okay, thank you for all your hard work, everyone. I think we're making progress. I know it's been a long day."

• • • •

BY THE TIME THEY GOT home, Erica was exhausted. She'd been awake since the early hours. It didn't help that she was growing another human and was exhausted anyway.

"I'll cook," Shawn offered. "Something nutritious."

"Screw nutritious," she said. "Give me something with cheese and carbs."

If she wasn't half-starved, she'd just crash into bed and sleep, but she knew she needed to eat. If she didn't, she'd be awake again at two a.m. and in the kitchen rummaging around for food.

They'd picked Poppy up on the way home. Now she was a little older, she was staying up later, so it didn't matter so much if she was ferried from her aunt's house to home after eight p.m.

Poppy sat at the dining room table, only half-heartedly going over some homework she hadn't yet done.

"Mum, after the baby's born, it's not going to be sharing my room, is it?"

Erica threw her daughter a bemused look. "No, of course not. Why do you say that?"

"Well, you said you were going to turn your office into a nursery, but it's exactly the same."

Erica laughed. "We've got a long time to go before the baby arrives, and when he or she does, they'll be in with me for the first few months." She grinned at Shawn. "Shawn might want to move in with you then, though. Anything to escape a baby crying all night."

Poppy rolled her eyes. "Shawn won't want to stay in my room. Anyway, it's too small."

"I know, love, I was only joking."

"Poppy is right, though," Shawn said. "Maybe we should start thinking about the nursery. We could put a daybed in there, too."

"So you *are* trying to escape," she teased.

He strained boiled pasta out into the sink and spoke with his back to them. "Might be handy for either of us when the baby moves in there and still needs night feeds. I promised you that I'd pull my weight, and I meant it."

She appreciated the sentiment, but unfortunately he was missing a couple of important appendages which meant she would be doing the bulk of the feeds, at least in the first few months.

"I still think there's no rush," she said. "There's plenty of time for decorating."

Was there another reason why she didn't want to create the nursery just yet? No, it was just too soon. It was normal to be cautious, especially at her age. It wasn't as though she was in her twenties anymore. The doctors had already run her through all the extra testing they offered because of her age, and the thought alone made her anxious. She wished she could be the super positive one in the family, but jumping in one hundred percent like Shawn felt like bad luck.

Besides, right now was hardly the right time to be thinking about it. They had a murder case on their hands. That was going to take all of her energy, and it wasn't as though she had much to start with.

Shawn conjured up a large serving of macaroni and cheese and a plate of salad. "Come on, sit down and eat."

She stifled a yawn behind the back of her hand. "Will you mind if I go and collapse in bed the moment I stop chewing?"

"Of course not," Shawn said. "We can manage, right, Poppy?"

"Does this mean I get to stay up later?" Poppy asked.

"Not too late," Erica warned.

Shawn ruffled Poppy's hair, and Poppy ducked away, running her fingers through the strands to smooth them. Erica had noticed how Poppy had been paying more attention to her appearance lately. She guessed it was only normal, but she still wished Poppy had more time to just be a little girl before jumping into the pre-teens. Having a new baby around would also make Poppy seem older than she really was, and Erica felt sad at the thought of her girl growing up too fast.

Erica finished eating and gave another wide yawn. "Okay, I'm going to hit the sack. That was delicious. Thank you. Don't worry about waking me when you come up. I'm pretty sure even a zombie invasion wouldn't get me out of bed at this point."

Shawn picked up her empty plate. "Let's hope it doesn't come to that."

Erica laughed and took herself up the stairs.

Chapter Thirteen

F rances drew in a deep breath, straightened her shirt, and then pushed into her publisher's office in Canary Wharf.

She loved this part of the city, with its tall glass towers and busy business people. There was such a vibrant, high energy to the place, especially in the summer when people emerged from their offices to eat and socialise in the sun. Technically, they were heading into autumn now, but the warm weather made it feel like it was still summertime. Though it was only just gone eight in the morning, the place thrummed with life.

She had a meeting with her editor about the most recent book she'd submitted, book seven in her crime series, *Seize the Dead*, though that was subject to change. In fact, most of the book was subject to change, and she currently had her heart in her throat, knowing that her editor, Blaire, was about to tell her exactly what those changes would be.

Changes, she could work with, she just prayed he liked the book overall. It was about a particularly gruesome serial killer who her crack team of detectives had set out to bring to justice, and she hoped Blaire didn't think she'd gone overboard.

She didn't know why these things intimidated her so much. It was as though she lived with the constant fear that everyone around her was going to find out she was a complete fraud and announce it to the world.

A part of her felt like she didn't have enough *grit* to write what she did. That people would see this mild-mannered woman in her thirties and scoff at her for even attempting to write dark, gritty fiction. She felt she would have been better off growing up in the slums or having had a darker backstory than her white, middle-class upbringing. Not that she would wish that life on anyone, and she had to remind herself that she was the author; she wasn't one of her characters. She didn't need to make herself more interesting by giving herself a tragic backstory, though some would say losing her parents when she had was enough.

Even so, it was something that niggled at her.

She caught the elevator of the high-rise building, standing shoulder to shoulder with people in expensive suits.

It only served to reinforce her imposter syndrome. She felt as though everyone was looking at her, questioning her reason for being there. She didn't belong. She wasn't good enough. There were plenty of authors who were far more successful than she was.

Stop it, Frances, she chastened herself. *People love your work. You have every right to be here.*

The doors pinged open, revealing the reception desk directly opposite, the sign and logo for the publishing house on a plaque above it. Frances checked in, and the receptionist led her down the hallway to Blaire's office.

"Frances!" Blaire exclaimed. He got to his feet and reached his hand out to shake hers. "So lovely to see you again. Thanks for handing in your latest book on time. You've got no idea how often I have to deal with people missing their deadlines."

"Of course," she said, taking a seat opposite him.

She couldn't imagine missing a deadline. Just the thought filled her with an intense anxiety. She was someone who planned exactly what they were doing almost every minute of every day, and that included her work. She sat at that computer and bashed out whatever words she needed, no matter what. Even when she was sick, she still forced something out of her, promising herself that even if it was terrible, she could go back and edit it when she was feeling better.

Her husband got frustrated by her rigidity. If he had an unexpected day off, then he wanted her to take the day as well. He argued that what was the point in having such a flexible job if she was never flexible with it? It wasn't as though she had a boss or an office to go into who would miss her. But she was her own boss, and sometimes she thought she held herself to account far more strictly than anyone else would.

"How are you?" she asked.

Blaire had lost an uncle he was close to only a couple of months earlier, and it had hit him hard.

"Better," he said. "Thank you for asking. How did the signing go yesterday?"

"Well. There was a decent turnout, and everyone was very friendly."

She tried not to think about the man who'd been lurking at the back. Why was that playing on her mind so much? She knew she had a habit of obsessing over things. Normally it was her health, but the murder that was so similar to one she'd written in her book, combined with the strange atmosphere she'd sensed from the man at the signing, had given her something new to focus on.

She did her best not to be intimidated by all the framed book covers on the walls declaring awards for one million copies sold, or prestigious crime writer awards. She'd never won anything like that and doubted she ever would. She told herself it was enough that she supported herself with her work.

He threw her a smile. "Can't ask for more than that, right? Hopefully you've got some new loyal fans out of it. Having those readers who will pick that new book up on release day is what'll drive the book up in the charts."

She gave a small smile. "I hope so."

"Have you been making any plans for the next book? I know you've only recently submitted the last one, but it's best not to let things get stale."

"Of course. I've always got ideas. It's just trying to pin down the right one that's the problem."

"Well, I'm looking forward to hearing more about it. Murder is big business."

Frances gave a small laugh and glanced down at her hands. "Did you hear about that murder off Mile End Road?"

She felt a little stupid mentioning it to him, but she needed someone else to listen to her. It had been playing on her mind all day, and the more she thought about it, the more convinced she became that it had been taken straight out of one of her books.

He pursed his lips. "I heard a body had been found. A young man, is that right? The police are asking for anyone who might have seen or heard something to come forward." His eyebrows pinched, and he leaned his forearms on the table and edged closer. "You didn't see or hear anything, did you?"

She shook her head, her cheeks warming. "Oh God, no. Nothing like that. I just couldn't help thinking about one of my books."

His forehead furrowed, and he sat back. "One of your books? Why?"

"Don't you remember how the killer murders his victims in *A Perfect Death?* He impales them on spikes."

"Oh, right."

She could tell by his expression that he still didn't quite understand what she was talking about. "It just seemed freakishly similar to what happens in the book—this young man's murder, I mean. The way it was done. Even the age and description of the victim seemed similar. Don't you remember?"

"I'm sorry, I read so many, they all start blurring into one." He gave a soft chuckle, and she knew he was just humouring her. "People have been impaling others on spikes for hundreds of years. Look at Vlad the Impaler. Pretty sure he was the one to start the trend."

She forced a smile. "Yes, of course. It just rang a bell, that was all."

He planted his palms on the desk. "So, let's talk about your new book. I loved it, naturally."

She let out a breath. "Phew."

"Saying that, there are a few tweaks we're going to need to make to bring it up to reader expectations."

She'd been expecting this, but it always felt like a sting. "Just tell me what you need, and I'll do it."

"That's what I love about working with you, Frances. You're always so..." He seemed to seek for the word. "Pliable."

She raised an eyebrow. "Pliable?"

"Accommodating. No ego. Honestly, some of the writers I have to work with act as though I'm trying to cut the pinky fingers off their babies when I suggest making some changes."

Once again, the imposter syndrome hit—that twist of anxiety in her stomach. Was she not fighting enough for her characters? Should she be a bit more of a diva? Did it mean she didn't care enough or wasn't a 'real' author? Frances did her best to shove these thoughts to the back of her mind so she could focus on what Blaire was saying. She did appreciate that she agreed with pretty much all of the points he was making. With his input, the end result would be a better book, and she couldn't really see any reason to push back on his suggestions other than to be difficult, and that wasn't in her nature at all. She was a people pleaser, and all she really wanted was a quiet life where she could spend time with her fictional friends and then time with her real-life husband.

They ran through some of his suggestions, and then he glanced at his watch. "Well, it's been lovely to see you again. I'll look forward to hearing more about your new ideas."

It was clear the meeting was over. She gathered her handbag up and got to her feet. "Good to see you again, Blaire."

"You, too."

He walked her to the door, and she made her way on her own through the rest of the office to the bank of elevators. She smiled at those she caught the eye of, still feeling self-conscious.

She didn't like being in the lift. Too claustrophobic. She overanalysed every noise and bump and jolt, her pulse racing, waiting for something to go wrong. But nothing did, and it deposited her on the ground floor.

She hurried through the lobby and stepped outside, turning her face up to the sunlight.

Everything is fine, she reassured herself. Her editor liked her book.

So, what was wrong? Why did she have this annoying niggly feeling in the pit of her stomach that tried to tell her something wasn't quite right? She imagined it would be the same sense her long-ago ancestors might have felt when they were going out of their cave to hunt, only for some instinct to tell them it wasn't safe because there was a sabre-toothed tiger lurking just out of sight, ready to pounce.

She was being dramatic. There was no tiger waiting to eat her. She was standing in a bustling business district, surrounded by people and towering office blocks and luxury apartments, all beside the River Thames. It was just news of the murder that had bothered her, but it wasn't as though she hadn't heard of people being killed before. This was London, and the crime rate was high. Her last delve into researching her book told her that there had been over one hundred murders in the city just last year. So why was this one particular crime bothering her so much? She was fully aware she had an overactive imagination—she wouldn't be able to do her job without it—but this felt like more than her just imagining things.

The sudden certainty that someone was watching her hit hard, and she spun around, her heart racing. Her gaze searched the crowds, trying to spot someone who might have been paying her more attention than everyone else. The memory of the man at the signing jumped into her head. Why had she thought of him? Did she think he was here, too? Had her subconscious spotted him?

Frances forced herself to take a breath. With her hands clenched by her sides, she closed her eyes briefly and did her best to centre herself. She didn't want to spiral into a panic attack, especially not right outside her publisher's office, among all these people.

You're safe, you're safe, you're safe, she repeated in her head.

Gradually, the panic ebbed away.

She wished her husband was coming straight home tonight instead of seeing his brother.

Frances didn't think much of her brother-in-law, Pete. He was what people thought of these days as a player. It worried her that he'd lead Matt astray. She got the impression that he didn't think much of her either. He thought she'd tied Matthew down. Got in the way of their brotherly nights out.

They were polite to each other, for Matt's sake, and she'd never told Matt about the time his brother had tried to feel her up in a bar when she and Matt had only just got together. She convinced herself Pete hadn't known how serious they were becoming and did her best to put it to the back of her mind. Plus, Pete had been drinking. Maybe he hadn't realised who she was or had mistaken her for someone else. It was just a slip-up. Why she insisted on making excuses for this man, she wasn't sure, but she suspected it had something to do with her habit of not wanting to rock the boat.

She also hadn't wanted to put Matt in a 'it's me or him' situation, as she had a strong feeling that she would have been the one to lose.

Chapter Fourteen

Erica started the following morning with the usual roll call, catching up on any developments that might have happened overnight and making sure everyone knew what their actions were for the day.

There was still plenty to follow up on—hours of CCTV footage to go through and interviews with possible witnesses. They still hadn't tracked down everyone who'd got off the bus that night, including the man in his forties who Chelsea had said had been acting strangely. While plenty of people paid for the bus with pre-paid cards or apps on their phones, it seemed he'd used a handful of coins which meant he was harder to track down. Had he done that deliberately? With technology being what it was these days, most people left some kind of digital footprint wherever they went.

Jon spoke up. "I've found the footage of the run-in Taylor had with the bloke at the bar. I printed off some images." He got to his feet and handed one to Erica.

The image was in black and white, but it was clear enough.

The bloke at the bar looked like a tough nut. A shaved head and lots of tattoos. He was also bulked with muscle, which meant he was probably physically strong enough to overpower the victim, especially if the victim was drunk.

"I ran facial recognition footage on the image, and we got lucky," Jon said. "His name is Patrick Beam, thirty-six years old. He's got a record of violence. Grievous bodily harm and actual bodily harm. He's served time, a couple of short sentences between 2007 and 2015."

"That's interesting. Any luck on tracking him down?"

"We've got an address on a driver's licence. Not sure how up to date it is. I've only just got this information, so I haven't had a chance to check it out yet."

"Good work. Let's try to speak to him. Those past cases he was convicted for—any sign of him carving things into people's chests?"

What did the carved letter mean, though? Erica felt as though if the victim had been killed via taking a beating, then she could align it more with the idea that the death had been the result of a delayed bar brawl. But there was something more deliberate about the way the victim had been killed.

"No, nothing like that. Just good old-fashioned cases of beating people to a pulp."

Erica twisted her lips. "Still...maybe he's got a new MO. Is there any sign from the CCTV footage on the street to indicate this man followed Taylor?"

Jon shook his head. "Not so far, but I'm still going through it all."

"Okay, let me know." She turned her attention to the rest of the team. "How are we getting on with everything else?"

They filled her in on any details she might have missed. There was still no sign of whatever blade had been used to create the wounds on the victim's chest, and the area had been opened back up and the search called to a halt. That was frustrating.

"We got some information back from the phone company," Hannah said, "and got a ping for Taylor's phone off a cell tower shortly before midnight, but unfortunately, it only confirms what we already know about his location."

"There was nothing after he was killed?"

"No, sorry. Whoever took the phone most likely was aware it would be traced and destroyed it."

Erica considered this. "Why take it in the first place then?"

"Maybe it had something on it that would implicate them?"

"Which suggests Taylor knew the person who killed him."

• • • •

ERICA WAS BUSY AT HER desk for the next couple of hours. She checked with digital forensics about the laptop, but they still hadn't made any progress.

The new constable, Lewis Crowe, approached her. He seemed a little nervous of her. Was she really that snappy at the moment? Yes, she guessed she was.

"Boss, I've got another one of Taylor Quigley's friends asking to speak to you. I've put him in interview room two. His name is Leeroy Hall."

"Did he say what he wanted?" Erica asked.

The younger detective shook his head. "No, just that he wanted to speak to you about Taylor."

"Let's hope he's got some useful information for us. You want to sit in with me?"

This only seemed to make him more anxious, but he nodded. "Yeah, sure."

Erica rose from her desk, and Lewis followed along behind her.

They reached the interview rooms, and she punched in the code to let them in.

The young man sitting at the table appeared to be barely out of teenagerhood. A crop of acne spattered across his cheeks and chin, and beneath that was red scarring. Poor kid. In this day and age of filters and perfection, it couldn't be easy to go through life like that. He seemed nervous, his knees pressed together, his hands shoved in his pockets.

"Hi, Leeroy. I'm DI Swift, and this is DC Crowe, but I understand you've already met. I've been told that you wanted to talk to me about Taylor Quigley?"

The skinny lad nodded. "That's right. I didn't know if I should come in, but I saw the quotes in the news from Taylor's mum about what a good son he was, and it was bugging me that you might not have got a different point of view."

A different point of view? That implied Taylor wasn't as innocent as his mother had made out.

"Can we get you anything before we start?" Erica offered. "Coffee, water?"

"Nah, I'm fine.

"Do you mind if I record this?"

"I guess not."

Erica nodded over to Lewis to start the recording.

"Were you out with Taylor the night he was killed?" she asked.

"No, I had to work."

"What do you do for a job?"

"Nothing exciting. Working in a warehouse in Stratford. I drive the forklift and move boxes from one place to another. I often work nightshifts. The money is better."

"And how long have you known Taylor?"

"Years. We went to school together." He glanced down at the table as though he didn't want the detectives to see his eyes welling up. His face grew tight and pinched. "It fucking sucks that Taylor was killed like that. I can't believe that someone would do that to him."

"His mother said he wasn't the kind to get in trouble. But you believe different?"

"Taylor wasn't some angel like his mum thinks. I mean, he didn't get in trouble or anything, but he knew how to party."

"What do you mean, exactly, by party?" she prompted him.

The young man shrugged. "You know, he liked to go clubbing, and drinking, and...stuff."

"Drugs?"

"Nothing serious, but yeah. A bit of weed, ketamine, coke, ecstasy. That kind of thing."

That sounded like a lot of drugs to her, but she understood what he meant. Taylor had been using them to party, not because he was an addict.

"Did he ever have any problems because of the drugs? Any issues with dealers or owing money? That kind of thing?"

"Not that I know of, but that doesn't mean it isn't possible."

"Is there anyone else we could talk to who might know more details?"

His tongue swiped across his lower lip. "Not really. I guess you can ask some of the other guys, but I'm not sure they'd known any more than me."

"Do you know who he was scoring from?"

The young man glanced away and shifted uncomfortably in his seat. He blew out a breath. "I don't really want to go down that route. I don't want people to think I'm a rat—especially not those kinds of people. I mean, if you think one of them might have done that to Taylor..."

She held up a hand to stop him. "I'm not saying it might have been one of them. I simply want to make sure we've explored every avenue. Plus, I'm not interested in the drugs. That's not my job. What I want is to find Taylor's murderer and prevent them from ever hurting someone like that again."

His lips thinned, and he stared down at his hands.

"Anything you can give me might help," she pressed. "A name, a location?"

"I don't know much, but I think he went to a place somewhere off the Mile End Road."

"So near to where he was killed?"

"Maybe. It's a long road and could be either east or west. Like I said, I don't know much."

Erica remained silent, allowing him to fill the space with more information, but he didn't add anything else.

"Thank you for coming in, Leeroy," she said finally. "I realise it can't have been easy to speak about your friend, when your instinct was probably to protect him."

"I'd rather you caught the bastard who did it than worry about Taylor's reputation. Tay wouldn't have cared if people knew he did a bit of coke and shit, but he definitely would have wanted the fucker caught. He'd be so pissed knowing whoever killed him was still walking around out there."

She handed him her card. "If you think of anything else, please don't hesitate to get in touch, especially if you remember the location of the place Taylor scored from."

"Yeah, sure. I hope you catch who did this to him."

"We appreciate you coming to talk to us. My colleague can show you out."

Erica allowed Lewis to walk him out, while she returned to her desk. She beckoned Shawn over and filled him in on what she'd just been told.

"You think there's something in it?" he asked.

"I'm not sure yet. Could he have had a run-in with his dealer?"

"If a drug dealer was going to murder someone, they wouldn't be stupid enough to dump the body right on their own doorstep. They'd drive the body out to Epping Forest or dump it in the Thames. Not leave it on the railings for everyone to see."

Erica considered this. "Unless it was dumped on someone else's doorstep to make a point."

"Or Taylor was going there to score, and he happened to be in the wrong place at the wrong time, and this has nothing to do with drugs. I can't find any historic records where there's been a killing like this related to any gang or, in fact, that there's been a killing like this at all. Plenty of youngsters take recreational drugs. They don't all end up speared onto a railing and with a letter carved into their chests."

She let out a breath. "Very true. The question is, why did this one? Right now, drugs is the only motive we've got."

She was getting frustrated at the lack of progress. How did someone do that to another person and just walk away? Someone must have seen them or the vehicle they'd used to flee the scene. She couldn't imagine the perpetrator remaining on foot—the killer would have been covered in blood spatter. Unless they changed their clothes, in which case, what did they do with the old ones? It made sense that whoever was responsible had also had a vehicle that they'd used, but with no cameras on the road where the body had been found, and the main road being extremely busy, their chances of narrowing down exactly what vehicle they'd used was slim. Maybe they'd even changed their clothes and got onto the damned bus?

"We'll get to the bottom of it," Shawn reassured her.

Chapter Fifteen

Frances dropped onto the sofa, her lunch of a ham and cheese sandwich balanced on a plate in one hand. She'd changed out of the smart clothes she'd worn to her publisher's office and was now back in the leggings and oversized t-shirt she tended to live in when she was home.

She used the remote to put the local news on and set the plate down on the coffee table.

Frances winced and pressed her hand to the side of her breast, at the spot just before she reached her armpit. She'd been getting a stabbing pain all morning, and now she palpated the area anxiously, fearful of finding a lump. In her head, she thought it was only a matter of time. She was sure something was going to get her eventually. She felt around, concentrating hard, but didn't find anything. That didn't mean there wasn't anything there, though. Perhaps it was just too deep to feel? The pain was there for a reason. It was a warning sign—telling her to pay attention.

She felt sick at the thought. Her picture of the future warped to become one filled with hospital appointments and surgeries, of her losing her hair, and even her breasts. What would Matt think of her then? Would he stick around and take care of her, or would he run for the hills?

Her eyes filled with tears, and she gave herself a shake. Matt was more likely to leave her because of her crazy mind, not because of any physical illness she might have. She didn't know how he put up with her. She drove herself nuts, and he must have the patience of a saint not to have walked out on her already.

The serious voice of the male news reporter, in his sixties, filled her ears, distracting her.

"After the murder of a young man, who has now been identified as twenty-two-year-old Taylor Quigley, police are asking for anyone with information to come forward. Especially those around the area between midnight and two a.m...."

Where had she been while that was happening? At home, tucked up in bed, with Matt asleep next to her. She'd been nowhere near the area at the time, but did that mean she didn't have any information?

The police were asking directly. They wanted to know if people had information, which meant they didn't have any leads, didn't it? And she knew something, or at least thought she might.

In her book, *A Perfect Death*, the killer had been a man seeking out a person he'd believed had been having an affair with his wife. Anyone who vaguely resembled the man who'd cuckolded him had triggered him and led to a violent rage.

It was ridiculous to think the same motive applied here, but perhaps it would help the police in their investigations?

She tried to picture herself walking into a police station and telling them her suspicions. She imagined the expression on the officer's face, how he'd probably look like he'd only recently left school and would be doing his best to hide his mirth. He'd most likely tell his colleague, and they'd rib each other and have a laugh over it.

Was her embarrassment worth catching a killer, though?

No, she couldn't do it. It was just a coincidence, surely, like Matt said. She bet if she Googled people being killed on metal railings, this probably wouldn't be the first time, or the last. It was only because it was so physically close that she'd paid such attention to it.

She needed to stop thinking about it—it was taking up far too much of her headspace.

Frances picked up the remote control and switched the channel.

Chapter Sixteen

Jon Howard approached Erica after lunch.

"Boss, I've managed to speak with Patrick Beam. The driver's licence address was up to date."

"And?"

"He remembers the incident perfectly. He claims Taylor was drunk, and staggered into him, and made him spill his pint all down himself. Said he was pretty pissed off about it, and they exchanged words—or at least Patrick did. Taylor just wandered off again."

"Do we believe him?"

Jon shrugged. "Maybe. Obviously, Patrick Beam has a history of violence, but the problem is, he's got an alibi, at least according to him. He says he picked up a woman at the pub and spent the night at her place."

"And they went straight from the pub?"

"According to him, yes. We don't know who the woman is yet, though he's given us a vague address."

Erica raised an eyebrow. "He doesn't know her name? Not even a clue? Didn't take a phone number?"

"No, he says it was a one-night thing. That they both knew the score."

She let a long breath out through her mouth. "Sounds like we need to find the woman to verify the story. We still don't know what happened to Taylor in between leaving the pub and being found on the railings, but we've got maybe two hours missing. If the victim wasn't killed until a couple of hours later, would Beam have had enough time to go to this woman's flat, get his end away, and then leave? Maybe he happened upon the victim when he was leaving and seized the opportunity."

"It's possible. According to Patrick, she doesn't live far from where the victim was found. It's about fifteen minutes on foot. I'm sending uniform out to meet him to see if he can remember how to get there."

She arched an eyebrow. "He's willing to try?"

"If it means crossing him off a list of suspects for a murder, absolutely. He says he's a changed man from when he was younger. That he did anger management courses and it changed his life."

They'd see if that was true. After all, not everyone brutally murdered someone just because they'd had a run-in at the pub. Besides, there was something deliberate about the way Taylor had been killed. As well as being spiked on the railings, he'd also been branded with a knife or even a scalpel.

Where was the blade now? The searches around the area hadn't produced anything, so had the murderer kept the weapon on them? Why had they had it in the first place? Unfortunately, carrying a knife wasn't uncommon around here. Even though there were laws against it, and the police had done their best to get tougher on the crime in recent years, nothing they were doing seemed to hold back the tide, especially among the young. They convinced themselves they needed to carry one to defend themselves, but, just like with guns, carrying one only increased the chances of them becoming a victim of knife crime.

"Let's try to find the woman he had the one-night stand with then. Was she in the pub with him? I assume you got a description."

"Of course. I'll check the footage again."

"Thanks, Jon."

Erica still needed to follow up on the names of the workers that the owner of the dropshipping business had given her. It was possible they'd seen someone acting suspiciously around the area.

She'd taken the scrap of notepaper where Shawn had jotted down the numbers, and now she found it and smoothed it back out.

She called the first number only to get a tinny-sounding voice: *The number you have dialled has not been recognised.*

Erica narrowed her eyes. She tried the second one, only to get the same response. That arsehole, Heale, had given her incorrect numbers. Dammit. She should have taken them straight from his phone instead of letting him read them out. The bloke had seemed shifty, and she hadn't trusted her gut on that.

It was easy enough to find *his* correct number, though—that was the thing about running a business, people needed to be able to get hold of you.

He answered the phone with a gruff, "Yeah?"

"Mr Heale, it's DI Swift here. We met yesterday."

"How could I forget?"

"The numbers you gave us for those workers were wrong."

"Oh, were they? They must have given me the wrong numbers, too."

She let out a frustrated sigh. She didn't have time for this.

"You said you'd called them to tell them not to come in because of the road being closed. Don't bullshit me, Mr Heale.

Why don't you want us to speak to them? Is it just that you've been hiring people who shouldn't be working in this country?"

"I told you, I asked them if they were allowed to work, and they said yes."

"But you didn't get the necessary paperwork. There are two ways we can go here, Mr Heale. You can give me the correct numbers, or I can pass your name on to the Home Office, where they can issue fines of up to sixty grand, per worker, and send you to jail for five years. I expect we'll also be able to get a warrant to see if you have any other illegal immigrants on your property."

"This is ridiculous. They won't be able to tell you anything."

"I'm not interested in your business, Mr Heale. All I want is to find the person who murdered an innocent young man."

"Fine," he muttered. "You got a pen?"

"Yep. Ready whenever you are."

Chapter Seventeen

Erica got what she needed and finished the call, but before she got the chance to progress any further, her phone rang.

"DI Swift, it's Doctor Hamilton," the familiar voice on the other end of the line said. "I just wanted to let you know that I've finished the post-mortem of Taylor Quigley, and I've uploaded the report to the case file."

She pressed the phone to her ear. "I appreciate that, thank you. Did anything jump out at you that I should pay attention to?"

"I guess, unsurprisingly, the cause of death was definitely due to the spike in the back of his skull. It caused massive trauma and an intracranial haemorrhage which is what ultimately killed him."

"How long did it take him to die?" she asked.

He sucked in a breath. "From that kind of trauma, I'd estimate three to four minutes."

Jesus. Had the person who'd been responsible stood there and watched poor Taylor die? Had Taylor been aware of what had been happening to him?

Hamilton continued. "The tox report was interesting. He was definitely intoxicated. Blood alcohol level of nought-point-three, which is dangerously high. It would have made him vulnerable, and he possibly wasn't thinking straight. I also detected cannabis and ketamine in his system."

"So he wasn't just drunk, he was pretty out of it."

"Based on that report, I'd say so, yes."

Perhaps that had been a blessing. He might not have known what was going on.

Erica thanked Hamilton for the information and ended the call. She took some time to open up the case file and go over the report in detail, making sure there was nothing important they might have missed.

The rest of the afternoon flew past.

Towards the end of the day, DC Jon Howard got back to her about Patrick Beam's alibi.

"We've tracked down the woman Patrick Beam had spent the night with. Her name is Lola Spires. She's thirty-four years old and works as a lunch assistant in a local school. She confirms she was with him during the late hours of the evening and into the early hours of the morning. There's no chance Patrick is the one who murdered Taylor."

Dammit.

That was another lead they'd shut down then. She was pleased they weren't going to waste any more time on the wrong person, but it meant that they were at the end of the second day and back to square one.

Chapter Eighteen

It was the middle of the night, and Matt hadn't come home. Frances lay in bed, staring at the ceiling, trying not to let it bother her. He'd said he'd gone back to his brother's place after the pub, and they'd had a few drinks, and it hadn't seemed worth getting a taxi all the way back home again.

Now the empty space in the bed beside her was like a yawning chasm that threatened to drag her in.

She tossed and turned, imagining all the possible scenarios which might have led to him deciding not to come home.

She told herself that she trusted her husband. She *had* to trust him. They were married, and trust was one of the most important foundations of a good marriage. But it was the brother she didn't trust. If Matt had been a bit drunk, could he have joined in when Pete decided that they should chat up a couple of young women at the bar? She pictured Matt telling himself that he was just acting as a wingman for his brother, and that there was no harm in talking, but then he'd end up being attracted to one of the women, and after he'd had a few drinks, they'd get close. She pictured Pete encouraging Matt, too, egging him on, and a slow rage burned inside her.

Maybe she was too sensitive. She was in her thirties now, and she was definitely starting to notice some fine lines where there hadn't been any before, and her body wasn't quite as slim and tight as it had once been. They hadn't had children—they'd both said they liked their lives as they were—but now she was starting to worry that Matt might change his mind one day, and she'd be too old to give him any. If that happened, he was bound to want a younger model.

Matt liked to take care of himself and spent a lot of time in the gym. Recently, that had been bothering her, too. She kept thinking about all the gym bunnies in their TikTok-influenced yoga pants that went right into their butts, and their tiny tops, taking selfies in the mirror.

What if he'd caught the eye of one of those women?

Frances groaned and covered her face with her hands. She didn't like this person she was becoming. She'd never been insecure or paranoid before. She'd always believed there was far more to her than just her body. It was her mind and heart that he loved.

They were happily married, weren't they?

She rolled over in the bed again, her foot straying into the spot where her husband was supposed to be. She was being dramatic—he was allowed to stay away for a night, and it wasn't as though he hadn't told her where he was.

So what was it that was bothering her so much?

She didn't like being alone in the house either. Though they lived in a fairly nice area, she was always conscious of making sure her doors and windows were locked at night. There was a small square opposite, surrounded by the same black metal railings that had inspired a certain scene in a book, that was pretty and inviting in the daylight. There were benches where old people and mothers with prams sat to pass the time of day, and carefully maintained borders and corners of grass. But, at night, a different kind of person could often be found there, gangs of youths drinking and getting high, or homeless people searching for a bench to sleep on.

She knew she shouldn't judge, but it still made her uncomfortable when she was home alone.

With a sigh of frustration, Frances threw off the covers and swung her legs out of bed. She wasn't going to sleep, so she might as well get up and make a cup of tea and do some work.

Blaire had emailed her the book file back so she could run through what changes he wanted to be made. Hopefully, there wasn't going to be anything that would require rewriting big chunks of it. She already had the storyline for the next book buzzing in her head, asking to be written, and she much preferred moving on to something new than going back over old territory. Still, it was part of the job.

At least she didn't have anything to get up for. She didn't need to go into an office or do a school run. They didn't even have a dog she needed to walk.

Instead of taking comfort in those thoughts, she suddenly found herself feeling completely adrift. What did she have, other than Matt and her work?

She hadn't even seen her old friends in forever. They all either had children now, and always seemed to be busy with kids' birthday parties or swimming lessons or something of the like, while those who hadn't yet started a family had emigrated to Australia or America.

A wave of depression washed over her. She had her career, but that could be taken away at any moment if her publisher decided not to renew her contract. Then all she'd have was her imagination—talking to her imaginary friends with no one to read their stories.

Frances went into her kitchen, flicked on the light, put fresh water in her kettle, and set it to boil.

The kitchen window had a view of the back garden, but all she could see was her own reflection staring back at her. She tugged her dressing gown tighter around her body and smoothed down her hair. She was a mess, but what did it matter? It wasn't as though there was anyone else here to see her.

Beyond her reflection, something moved.

Frances froze, her heart suddenly beating hard and fast.

Beside her, the kettle rumbled and bubbled and then clicked off, but she had forgotten all about the tea. Her gaze was locked on the darkened area outside her kitchen window. Was her back door locked? Was the front? She was sure she'd double-checked them before she'd gone to bed last night. She was always more cautious when Matt wasn't home. Though she never thought of herself as being famous, she was certainly in the public eye more than she would be if she worked a regular nine-to-five. She always took whatever steps she could to ensure that she kept her privacy, but it wasn't easy, especially in this day and age of people being able to use computers to find out pretty much whatever they wanted.

Had it been a fox? There were plenty of them around. She heard them fighting at night—some god-awful noises they made. But her instincts told her this hadn't been a fox. It hadn't slunk, low to the ground, in the way that foxes did. It had been bigger and had darted away, as though it had been aware that it had been seen.

If only she hadn't turned the light on when she'd entered the room, she would have seen whatever—or whoever—had been outside, and they wouldn't have seen her.

With a shaking hand, she took a couple of steps backwards, reaching for the light switch again. While she didn't want to stand in the dark, she also needed to see more clearly than staring at her own reflection.

Her fingers met with the brushed brass light switch Matt had insisted they install, rather than the boring white plastic ones, and she flicked the light off again.

The garden was empty.

She wished Matt was here. Why couldn't he have come home last night instead of staying out? But then she realised that if he had come home, she'd have slept like a baby and wouldn't be downstairs at three a.m. staring out of her kitchen window. She wouldn't have been any the wiser.

Frances tried to remember if she'd heard of any break-ins around the area recently. There were gangs of young men who scouted housing estates, trying door handles and cars, hoping to find one unlocked so they could steal whatever was inside. Whoever had been in her back garden might have been one of those people.

But then she remembered how she'd felt after she'd come out of her publisher's office, that sense of someone's gaze being on her. Immediately, her brain then made the connection with the man at the signing.

Could it be the same one?

She was being paranoid. Writing crime, it came with the territory. She always saw the nefarious in the everyday and let her imagination get away with her. Perhaps it had just been a fox, and the distortion from the window reflection had made it look bigger.

"It doesn't matter," she said to herself. "You're safe in here. No one is getting in."

She repeated the mantra to herself in her head: *You're safe, you're safe, you're safe.*

It was something she'd started doing when her issues with health anxiety had taken over. The brain was an interesting thing. It didn't know the difference between reality and her imagination, which meant that when she fed it all the negative thoughts around her believing she was going to die, her brain sent her body into a panic, believing those thoughts to be true. In reverse, telling her brain the opposite—that it was safe—should rewire it to believing *that* to be the truth.

Her health anxiety had got worse as she'd got older.

Frances's mother had died of breast cancer when Frances had only been seventeen, and then, only a year later, she'd lost her dad from a heart attack. It had come out of nowhere. Her dad had always been a reasonably fit man—took care of himself and played sport regularly. It had happened during his weekly Wednesday evening football game, something he'd jokingly described as football for old men, even though he'd only been in his early sixties. Even that, it seemed, had been too much for him. He'd collapsed and died before the ambulance had even been called. It had come as such a shock for Frances that she hadn't been able to believe it at first. She'd thought it was some kind of twisted joke.

When had her health anxiety started? She couldn't even say for sure, but she believed it had been after her mum had died, or had she been fine until her dad's passing? She thought anyone who'd lived with cancer in their lives, even if it was via a loved one, automatically made you more conscious of that wicked disease. Frances had checked her breasts for lumps far more regularly, but she was sure that was only normal, and probably a good thing. Perhaps if her mum had checked more regularly, they'd have caught it before it spread. But then the checking became more than just her breasts. A pain in the stomach must be a tumour. Loose stools must have meant bowel cancer.

Her heart beating too fast immediately brought to mind her father's heart attack, and, instead of calming her down, only made her more panicky, which in turn, increased her heart rate.

The problem was that she could never escape from her body, or from her own mind. The only time she didn't really think about it was when she was writing. Then she could put her fears into the characters instead.

It had been the suddenness of her father's death that had been the worst part. At least with her mum, they'd had time to talk—to say goodbye. With her dad, he'd been there one minute, and then simply just gone. It made her feel as though she couldn't trust that there would be a tomorrow.

If she went to bed with a headache, she'd be frightened to fall asleep in case she had an aneurysm during the night and never woke up.

A pain in her leg instantly became a life-threatening blood clot.

Matt told her she should see a doctor about it, that they could put her on medication to help control her anxieties, but she didn't want that either. She told him she was fine, that she didn't want to take pills for something when she wasn't actually ill. What she didn't tell him was that she was worried that if she took medication then it would disguise her symptoms if she did ever get sick. What if she was about to have a brain aneurysm but she didn't take note of the warning signs because she was too spaced out on some drug or another?

She also worried that medication like that might affect her writing, and right now, her writing was all she had.

Still in the dark, Frances made her cup of tea, the whole time feeling as though someone was standing outside her window, watching her. She wished she had a blind she could pull down, but they'd never bothered to install one since the kitchen wasn't overlooked at all. She wasn't going to allow either her overactive imagination, or some random fox, chase her out of her own kitchen.

She didn't miss the tremble of her hand as she plucked the teabag out of the cup and added a splash of milk. She'd been planning on working, but now she didn't think she'd be able to concentrate on anything like edits. Instead, she carried the mug into her living room, set it on her coffee table, and then curled up on the sofa. She tugged down the throw that was folded on the back of the furniture and covered her legs.

She'd stay that way until the first hint of daylight bled into the sky.

Chapter Nineteen

The following morning, Erica and Shawn paid a visit to the address she'd got for the two people who worked for Luke Heale who were originally from Poland.

Both of Mr Heale's employees lived in an old council flat in a block in Stratford. The address was on the fourth floor, and they had to get an external lift, which stank of urine and stale booze, to the openair walkway that ran past the front doors.

"You know we could have sent Jon and the new guy to do this," Shawn said as they searched for the correct flat number.

"Yeah, I know," Erica replied. "Maybe I'm just being petty because I don't like that arsehole Heale, but something tells me there's more to this than Heale hiring people he shouldn't." She slowed her walk. "I think this is the place."

Groups of people were hanging around outside. Different languages blended together in a background hum, and skin tones varied from pale to dark. Like most of London, this area really was a cultural melting pot. Numerous people—far too many to be occupying the three-bedroom flat—appeared to be staying at the address.

One of the men glanced in their direction and caught Erica's eye.

"We're looking for Alicija and Konrad?" she said. "Are they here?"

He gave a shrug of a shoulder and jerked his head towards the interior of the flat. "Alicija?" he yelled.

The front door stood open, and Erica caught the unmistakable smell of weed.

A petite blonde girl, probably no more than twenty, if she was even that, appeared in the doorway. She caught sight of Erica and Shawn and started back in fear. Her head darted from side to side, as though she was searching for an escape route, but they were four stories up, and Erica and Shawn were blocking the way.

Erica put out her hand. "It's okay. You're not in any trouble. We just want to talk to you about something that happened near Mr Heale's dropshipping business. You know Mr Heale?"

The girl nodded.

"Is there somewhere we can talk?" Shawn asked.

Seeing she didn't have much choice, the girl led them into a small living room. From the rolled-up mattresses in the corners, it seemed as though people were using the living room to sleep in, too. One of the walls was painted bright red, and pots of ferns and other foliage were positioned on every surface. A door led out onto a narrow balcony.

They all took seats on the two sofas that looked like they'd been rescued from skips.

"Can I take your full name?" Erica asked.

"Alicija Nowak," the girl replied in a small voice.

"How long have you been in the UK?"

"Not long. Only a couple of months."

Erica offered her a smile, wanting to get her onside. "Your English is very good."

"Thank you. I studied in Poland."

"You're working for Mr Heale, is that right?"

She didn't meet Erica's eye. "Yes, that is right."

"How long have you been working for him now?"

"Only six weeks maybe."

Immigration wasn't Erica's job. It was only because this business might be linked to the murder that she was asking these questions. But deep down, she felt like something was off, and not just because this woman clearly wasn't supposed to be working here. It ran far deeper than that.

Erica wasn't about to get into an argument about the state of illegal immigration in the country. The whole thing was one big mess as far as she could tell. But she also didn't like people like Heale who took advantage of vulnerable people so he could line his pockets.

"Do you recognise this man?" She showed her a photograph of the victim.

The young woman stared at it. "No, I am sorry. I do not know him."

"Okay, thank you." Erica tucked her phone away. "Were you working the day before yesterday?"

The woman gave a brisk nod as a response.

"Did you see anyone or anything unusual around the area where you work over the last few days? Anyone hanging around?"

Her lips pursed. "No, I don't think so."

"Has Mr Heale had any problems with anyone?"

"I really do not know anything about Mr Heale or his problems."

There was tension in her tone.

"What's Mr Heale like?" Erica asked.

"He is okay."

"Do you ever see strange people coming and going from the yard?"

She shook her head quickly but still didn't meet Erica's eye.

"What kind of business does he run from the containers?"

Her words were stilted, overpronounced and cautious. "He sells lots of different things. It changes all the time."

Erica got the impression she was trying to be careful not to say the wrong thing.

"How does he treat you? Is he a good boss?"

Erica couldn't imagine any world where he would be a good boss.

Alicija shrugged. "He is okay." But she pulled the sleeve of her shirt down, subconsciously covering something.

Erica frowned and leaned forward. "What's on your wrist, Alicija?"

Her lips tightened. "Nothing."

"Can you show me? I want to help you." Erica was sure she'd caught sight of bruises around the girl's painfully thin wrist, bruises that looked suspiciously like fingerprints. "Is someone hurting you?"

The girl tugged her sleeve down again. "It's nothing."

Erica couldn't imagine how hard life must have been to make her want to leave her own home and family, only to find herself living in squalor and working for a man like Heale. She experienced a pang of guilt for feeling less than satisfied with her own life.

The living room door opened, and a young man entered. He paused in the doorway, his gaze darting between the three of them sitting there.

"Are you Konrad?" Shawn asked him.

The man ignored Shawn's question and instead addressed Alicija, speaking in a language Erica didn't understand. The girl snapped back at him, her words like gunfire. It was clear they weren't agreeing on something.

"What did you just say?" Erica asked Alicija, but it was the man in the doorway who replied.

"I told her that she should tell you," he said.

"Tell me what?"

"About the man she works for. That man is an arsehole who exploits vulnerable people and makes them do things they shouldn't. It's not only clothes and kitchenware that he sends out. He hides other things in the items."

"What kind of other things?" Erica pressed.

The girl twisted her hands in her lap. "Packets of white powder."

Erica held back from punching the air. Drugs. She knew there was more to Heale's business than he'd let on. Trouble was, would he be stupid enough to leave anything on site now the cops were sniffing around? Any sensible person would get anything incriminating far away from the site. Could he be considered a sensible person, though? He had that cocky demeanour that shouted that he didn't think anyone would touch him. Would that make him stupid enough to leave evidence on his property?

During her time on the force, she'd had many experiences of criminals doing stupid things. In fact, it was one of the things she could depend upon.

So this arsehole was using a dropshipping business as a front for his drug business—most likely cocaine. Maybe he had a keyword that he got people to use when they placed an order, something random so it wouldn't get mixed up with something else—and, if he saw it on the order, he'd know to include a packet of white powder alongside their order of boxer shorts or inside an insulated mug. She guessed that if he got caught, he'd blame one of the illegal immigrants he had working for him, saying they'd been the one to pack the order—which they most likely had been.

What did this all have to do with the man killed on the railings, though? Was it connected? Or was it just bad luck that the killer happened to choose that spot to puncture a man through the base of his skull? When she'd first spoken to Heale, he hadn't seemed particularly shaken up. Nothing he'd said or done had indicated to her that he'd believed the man had been left there as a threat. At the most, he'd simply seemed irritated at the disturbance.

Taylor Quigley's friend, Leeroy, had said Taylor liked to party, and Taylor had been intoxicated when he'd died. Had he been going to Heale's property, hoping to score, maybe forgetting that he normally did so via mail? No one had been there, of course, but had Taylor known that? Perhaps he was hoping to catch someone still around at that time of night?

So *was* Taylor killed because he'd been trying to score? Perhaps by a rival dealer, and then his body left as a message to Luke Heale? Or had someone already been following him, and that he'd been killed in that location had nothing to do with Heale and his business?

But wouldn't a man like Heale have plenty of enemies? She'd bet he'd left a trail of pissed-off people in his path. But then why hurt Taylor Quigley and not the man himself? So far, she hadn't found any connection between the two of them except that Taylor liked to party and, potentially, Heale liked to supply.

The Met no longer had a specific drug squad, but she knew DI Julian Colgan had been working this area. Maybe he knew of some links. He might also want in on the raid when she got the warrant through.

They were going to need physical evidence. She doubted the employee would testify, and, even if she did, a good defence solicitor would tear her to shreds on the stand. Immigration was a polarising issue, and an immigrant who'd been helping to post packets of coke all over the UK wouldn't be looked upon too kindly by a jury. That was even if they could get her on the stand, which Erica doubted would happen.

"What about the man you work with," Erica asked. "Konrad? Do you know when he'll be back?"

Alicija shook her head. "I have not seen Konrad since the morning Mr Heale phoned and said for us to not come in. Maybe he found work somewhere else. Or maybe he knew there was going to be trouble and did not want to get caught up in it."

Erica exchanged a glance with Shawn. So this Konrad did a runner the same morning the body had been found?

"What do you know about Konrad? Did you know him before you came to the UK?"

"No, I did not. But everyone tends to gather in their own communities here, you know? He was the one who told me about the job. I needed to work because I have no money."

"Did he tell you exactly what the job entails?"

Alicija picked at dry skin around her nails. "No, but he said not to ask too many questions and just do as I was told. It was not like I had many choices."

"What is Konrad's surname?"

"He says it is Budny. I do not know if it's the truth or not."

"Do you have any idea where he might have gone? Does he have any other contacts in London or any other parts of the UK?"

"He has said to me before that he knows people in Manchester, but I do not know if he would have gone there."

The fact was, there was little chance of them tracking down Konrad Budny. He wasn't in the system, which meant, other than the phone number, which was most likely a burner phone since he wouldn't have been able to get a contract, they had no way of tracing him. They didn't even know for sure that Konrad Budny was his real name. It was clear he'd sniffed trouble and made himself scarce.

Unless he'd been the one to kill Taylor.

"Okay. If you hear from him, or you get wind of anyone else knowing where he is, would you contact us?" She handed over her card. "He might have important information that could help us?"

Would Alicija stick around? Erica doubted she'd hear from her. She'd probably take off as well. She could take her in, but what would be the point? The girl would most likely clam up and deny everything or say she'd been lying. They had no physical proof to link her to the site, and she had been paid in cash, so at the most they probably had a few phone calls linking her to Heale. Keeping her onside was a far better way to play things.

Erica thanked Alicija again and then she and Shawn left the flat, winding between all the people still hanging around. Would any of them know where Konrad had gone? From the looks they were giving her and Shawn, she thought it highly unlikely any of them would tell them even if they did.

They caught the lift, Erica holding her breath against the smell, back to ground level, and headed back to the car.

"Think we've got enough to get a search warrant on Heale's place?" Shawn said.

"With that information, plus the fact a man's body was found hanging off the adjacent railings, yeah, I'd say so. If we find something, we might just get the charge to stick, too. Problem is, what the hell does this all have to do with Taylor Quigley's murder?

Had the motive been drug related?

Right now, it was the only lead they had.

Chapter Twenty

Frances hadn't been able to focus all morning. She'd had a lump in her throat every time she'd tried to swallow, and now her brain buzzed with anxiety at the possibility it was something more sinister than a bout of acid reflux caused by her overconsumption of coffee.

Matt had sent her a 'good morning' text, letting her know he was going straight into the office from his brother's place and checking that she'd had a good night. She replied that she'd missed him and hadn't slept well, but didn't go into the whole 'I thought I saw someone in the garden' thing. She already knew he'd be dismissive of her fears, and now, in the daylight, she found herself questioning what she'd seen, too. Had she just let her overactive imagination get away with her? She'd already been worrying, and the light had been on in the kitchen, making it hard to see outside. Perhaps it had just been her own reflection moving that she'd seen?

This was one of those days where she wished she had a regular office job to go to. Though she knew she'd be exhausted if she had to get on the Tube and sit at a desk all day, at least she'd be surrounded by people. She longed for the chatter of work colleagues, the offer of someone else to make her a cup of coffee, the sense of community that came with it.

Instead, she was in her house, facing a whole day alone with only her own self-imposed routine. It would be any of those office workers' idea of luxury, but right now she felt overwhelmed by the solitude.

Grief suddenly hit her, a fresh wave of longing for something that was impossible. She wished her mum and dad were still alive, that she could pop around there and tell them all her fears, and they'd make her a cup of tea and listen and give her a hug.

A tear spilled down her cheek. It had been almost fifteen years since she'd lost them, but she still missed them terribly. How adrift it felt to be a person without a parent, even at her age.

She needed to work on her edits and then she'd maybe take a hot bath or have a nap. Her eyes were gritty from the lack of sleep, but she knew she wouldn't sleep yet, even if she tried.

Feeling impossibly alone, she decided to try Matt on the phone. Hearing a friendly voice would help, she was sure. He'd reassure her that she had nothing to worry about.

Using her mobile phone, she swiped the screen for his number and hit 'call'.

He answered after only two rings. "Hi, love. I need to be quick, I'm about to go into a meeting."

Immediately, she felt shunned. "Oh, right. It's nothing in particular. Just wanted to see if you had a good night?"

She wouldn't tell him that she'd spent the whole night picturing him chatting up some young blonde or seething with hatred and resentment at his brother for taking him away.

"Yeah, it was fine. Food was a bit shit, but it lined the stomach. How was your evening?"

"It was fine, too," she lied. "Nothing too exciting happened. Are you going to be home for dinner?"

"Yeah, should be. I'll let you know if anything comes up." He paused and then said, "Look, love, I've got to go. I'll see you after work."

"Sure, love y—"

She didn't get to finish her sentence. He'd already gone.

With a sigh, she put down the phone. He'd sounded normal, hadn't he? But then, what did a man sound like if he'd spent a night with another woman? Would he sound any different?

Frances squeezed her eyes shut and then massaged her temples with her fingers, trying to ease the lingering headache that had burrowed its way into her skull. Matt had given her no reason for her not to trust him. Maybe he could be a bit dismissive sometimes, but she knew she wasn't easy to live with. Her anxiety made life difficult, and she told herself that it was proof that he really did love her that he put up with it. Yes, they had a ridiculously huge mortgage together, and London house prices were crazy, but that was hardly enough reason to stay.

Maybe she'd cook him a nice dinner, remind him why he should come home to her. Instead of acting paranoid and crazy, she'd be the perfect wife. He'd said the meal last night had been bad, so she'd pop to the supermarket and pick up a couple of steaks—fillet for her and a ribeye for him. She wouldn't mention her fears of him cheating on her, or that she'd thought she'd seen someone in the garden in the middle of the night.

The familiar clatter of her letterbox distracted her. She hadn't heard the postman arrive, and it was a bit late for him, too.

Frances went to her front door to retrieve the post. Instead of an envelope, she discovered a folded piece of paper with her name handwritten on the front. Had one of the neighbours delivered it to her? Maybe they were complaining about something—her parking or the way they'd put the bins out. That was the trouble with people these days. No one thought to just come and have a polite chat about a grievance. They preferred to leave notes on car windscreens, or, even worse, post something passive-aggressive on social media. Frances never understood why people did that. It wasn't as though whoever the post was aimed towards would ever see it, so their behaviour wouldn't change, and the annoyance would continue. She assumed it was just their way of venting.

With a frown, she opened it up and read the letter.

Dear Ms Gilchrist,

I just wanted to let you know how much I admire you. You and your words are such an inspiration to me. Please keep writing your wonderful books.

All the best,

Your number one fan.

Frances stared at the writing. There was nothing threatening about it. If she'd received it as an email, she'd have smiled and typed back a friendly reply, thanking them for getting in touch. Instead, all she could think of was that Stephen King book and movie, where a woman had kidnapped her favourite author and cut off his leg—or had she just broken it? She thought it differed between the movie and the book, as these things so often did.

She shook her thoughts away from the fictional and forced herself to focus on the very real letter in her hand. The paper trembled in her fingertips. One main thought yelled inside her head.

Someone knows where I live!

The letter had been hand posted, so not only did they know her address, they'd been on her very street. Had stood outside her door. Had pushed a note through her letterbox. That a person had been so physically close to her unnerved her. They'd been right outside the door only moments ago.

Frances rushed to her living room window and pressed her face to the glass. Frantic, she searched for any sign of someone lurking around, or even walking away, but the street was empty.

Could the person she'd seen in her back garden also be the same one who'd slipped the letter through her door? The new niggle of worry squirmed away inside her.

Could she take this letter to the police? What would they say? She couldn't see them doing anything; in fact, they'd probably laugh her out of the station. But what if she told them about the murder, as well, how it fit with one of the stories in her books? Frances covered her face with her hands. Even in her own head it sounded ludicrous. They'd probably think she was crazy and a time-waster. Her own husband had thought she was nuts when she'd tried to talk to him about it.

The letter felt like a time bomb about to explode in her hand. She wanted to screw it up and throw it away, but something told her that she might need it.

Frances just wanted to curl into a ball and cry.

Chapter Twenty-One

E rica had spoken to DI Julian Colgan, and he'd confirmed that they'd been trying to track down a source of cocaine that they believed had come from the local area, but that they hadn't been able to pin down the distribution location.

Together, they put a team in place, including a drug dog and his handler, and now they gathered on either end of the street where Luke Heale's dropshipping business was located.

They'd let a team of uniformed officers go in first, led by Sergeant Jo Banks, who would present Mr Heale with the warrant.

Heale had noticed the commotion and had stepped out of his office. He had the expression of a bulldog chewing a wasp and stood with his hands on his hips, glaring at all the police cars.

He hadn't made any attempt to run, however, or even lock up.

Erica was more than aware he might be prepared for this. With the attention brought to his business from the body being found, plus him knowing she had spoken to at least one of his—most likely now ex—employees, meant he could have taken steps to ensure their search came up empty-handed. But people like Heale made mistakes, and even if he thought he'd moved everything incriminating, it still didn't mean that they wouldn't find anything.

Because it was the middle of the day, the chain-link gates that separated the business from the street stood open. That would certainly make their job a bit easier.

They were gathering the attention of other passersby, too. Uniformed police asked them to move on, but some just took a few steps away and loitered, not wanting to miss out on something exciting.

"What the fuck do you lot want?" Heale called out to them.

Erica tried not to let her opinion of him show on her face. This guy was such an arsehole. She'd picked it from the start. Maybe the drugs and the illegal workers weren't connected to the murder, but he was still breaking the law. The worst part was that she was sure he wouldn't learn. He'd take whatever light sentence he got, and then get out of prison and start up all over again. He'd already proven that much by the number of businesses he'd had that had failed, only for him to leave a trail of debtors behind him, just to begin again in a different name. It shouldn't be allowed.

Now she wondered how many of those businesses had been fronts for even shadier work. He'd most likely been pushing drugs from them as well. Perhaps he'd shut them down because others had caught up with him who he didn't want to, and so it had been easier for him to move on than face up to whatever shit he'd got himself into.

"Mr Heale, we have a warrant to search these premises," Sergeant Banks called back.

"I don't give a fuck about your warrant."

Banks shrugged. "And I don't really care what you think. We have a right to be here."

"Don't you dare take one step onto my property."

Banks ignored him and did exactly that; two of her officers flanked her. She held up the warrant for him to see.

Heale glared at it, then snatched the paper out of her hand. He tore it into several pieces, threw them onto the ground, and finished with a glob of spit. "That's what I think of your warrant."

Banks didn't react. "I want every inch of this place gone over with a fine-tooth comb," she ordered her officers.

"The containers are all padlocked, Sarge," one of them said.

"Mr Heale," Banks asked, "do you have keys for the padlocks? It's either that or we'll have to cut them open, and I'm sure you won't want the cost of replacing them."

"Cut them. I'd rather cause you lot some hassle than worry about a few quid!"

"Suit yourself."

Sergeant Banks jerked her chin at her officers to tell them to go ahead.

Heale's gaze drifted past the officers and landed on Erica. "You're here, too, huh? I assume this is all your doing?"

Erica took a couple of steps forward. "This is my investigation, yes."

His lip curled in disgust. "Who the fuck do you think you are? Some trumped-up tart in a suit who thinks she's better than the rest of us?" He got right up in her face. "Fuck you."

Erica took a breath, forcing herself to remain calm. "Sir, I suggest you step away before I'm forced to arrest you."

"Arrest me? For what? I haven't fucking done anything. You know what you are? You're a fucking cunt. You deserve everything you get."

"What the fuck did you just say?"

Suddenly, Shawn was right there, using the bulk of his body to shove in between Erica and the man. "Get the fuck away from her."

Heale laughed. "Are you her little bitch?"

"Shawn, I can handle this," Erica said, stepping to one side of him.

Heale twisted towards her and lunged. He planted both hands on her shoulders and shoved.

She staggered away and somehow managed to fall over her own feet. She could feel herself going down but could do nothing to stop it. She didn't even manage to get her hands down to lessen the impact of the fall.

Erica landed hard on the concrete, her teeth snapping together, every bone in her body jarring. She'd hit her tailbone the worst, and pain radiated up through her spine. She lay there for a moment, trying to catch her breath and assess the damage.

From above her came a roar of anger.

"Motherfucker." Shawn went for Heale. "She's pregnant, you arsehole."

Other uniformed officers jumped in, half to drag Shawn off Heale, and half to help arrest Heale and pick Erica up off the ground.

"Are you okay?" one of the officers asked her.

There was a new kind of concern in his eyes, and she knew it was because of what Shawn had just said.

Erica couldn't believe he'd just said that. What the hell was he playing at, announcing that, not only to this piece of shit, but to all the officers who were here to support them?

She offered her hand to the officer, and he pulled her up to her feet. "I'm fine, thanks."

She dusted herself off. She'd have a bruised backside, but that was about all. It wasn't as though she'd broken anything.

Heale was facedown on the ground. Uniformed police yanked his hands behind his back, and cuffs snapped around his wrists.

"You do not have to say anything," the officer said, "but, it may harm your defence if you do not mention when questioned something which you later rely on in court. Anything you do say may be given in evidence."

Heale would be charged with assaulting a police officer as well as whatever they'd get him for after this search was complete.

Erica was fuming at Shawn, but right now she needed to be a professional. She glanced over her shoulder at the uniformed officers. They still had a job to do.

Her cheeks were still burning from Shawn's revelation.

"Congrats, DI Swift," one of the officers mumbled as he walked past.

She gritted her teeth. "Thanks."

This was the last thing she wanted. Now everyone would know. Gossip spread around the office like wildfire, and of course everyone would figure out the baby was Shawn's. She hated to think of all the jokes that would be made—both with her being slightly older than him and her being his boss. She wanted to go and hide in a corner and cover her face with her hands. Instead, she had to force herself to keep her head held high and get on with her job.

Shawn was by her side in an instant, his hand on her elbow. "Are you okay? Do you need to get checked out? I can drive you to the hospital."

She clenched her jaw and kept her voice to a hiss. "Jesus, Shawn, I'm fine. Don't make a fuss. We're at work."

"You went down hard. Are you sure you're not hurt?"

"I said I'm fine, didn't I? And I don't appreciate you making that announcement to the entire team."

He at least had the courtesy to glance down. "Sorry," he said. "It just kind of came out."

She couldn't look at him. "Yeah, I got that."

"I thought he was going to hurt you. Hurt the baby."

"I can take care of myself."

He pressed his lips together and stared at the ground. Christ, she'd known this was going to be a problem.

She closed her eyes briefly. "We'll talk about this later."

She walked away from him, needing some space, and tried not to wince as the movement sent further spikes of pain up through her lower back. It was just bruised—she didn't think she'd broken anything or she wouldn't be able to walk.

The team worked their way methodically through each of the metal shipping containers, allowing the drug dog to take his turn sniffing over each box. Did Heale have any kind of method as to how he had things organised? She assumed so, since it wasn't as though he could rifle through hundreds of boxes each time he needed to make a drop, but it wasn't as though he was going to impart that information to them.

She watched as the first of the containers were opened and the boxes searched, the drug dog sniffing through the contents. Though she'd got the warrant based on the possibility of drugs being present, she was also keeping her eyes open for anything that might be linked to the murder.

White polystyrene beads were everywhere. Boxes of short-sleeved t-shirts, yoga socks, and sports bars were followed by insulated mugs, and kids' lunchboxes, and milk frothers. It was like being at a car boot sale on steroids.

Shawn came to stand beside her. "Jesus, do people really buy all this crap online?"

"Sure they do. You're no one if you haven't got the latest water bottle." She remembered Poppy nagging her for one that she insisted everyone had, and, when she'd gone to look at the cost, had almost spat out her tea. "There's nothing illegal about selling this shit online, though. We need to keep going until we find something."

It was going to take some time to go through every box in every shipping container, and it was time Erica didn't have. She'd wanted to see the expression on Heale's face when they busted this place and also take him in for questioning. What else had he lied about, because he'd sure as hell tried to cover up that he'd been selling drugs from this place. He'd also lied the first time he'd given her the phone numbers of the people who'd been working for him.

At this point, she was struggling to believe a single word he said.

They had him cuffed in one of the police cars. A uniformed officer sat in the back with him.

"We're taking Heale down to the station to be processed," one of the constables told her.

"Okay, thanks. Put him in an interview room. Leave him to sweat a while."

"Will do." The constable paused and smiled. "And congratulations on your news."

Erica forced a smile. "Thanks."

Chapter Twenty-Two

They got back to the office a couple of hours later.

Erica was a little shaky after her confrontation with Heale, but she did her best not to let it show.

She went to fill DCI Gibbs in on what had happened. He listened to her, concern etched into his features, his fingers steepled at his lips.

"Do you need to be checked over by medical?" he asked when she'd finished.

"No, I'm fine, honestly. I went down hard, but I didn't damage myself."

His lips pursed. "What about this lead on the drugs? Is there a connection to the murder?"

"Honestly, at this point I'm not sure. It's possible Taylor was in the area hoping to score, but he doesn't show up on the CCTV. If he was heading that way, he was intervened before he got there."

Gibbs picked up a pen and flicked it between his fingers. "By the person who killed him?"

"Exactly." She went to cross her legs and then stopped as a spike of pain shot through her hip. "We've brought Luke Heale in for questioning, and we'll see what we can get out of him. Hopefully, the search teams will turn something up, but my gut tells me he was already prepared for our arrival and cleaned the place out."

Gibbs grimaced. "You're probably right about that. Any other leads?"

"Still working on it. We're waiting to hear back from digital forensics about the laptop. I'll let you know if anything changes."

Erica thanked him and left his office.

Shawn was waiting for her. "Did he tell you to go home?"

"No, why would he do that? I'm fine, and we're in the middle of a big case."

"Well, because..." His gaze darted down to her stomach.

Anger flared inside her. "Shawn, I don't want you treating me like I'm some fragile, precious jewel that needs protecting all the time." She knew she was snapping at him, but she couldn't help it. This was part of the reason she hadn't wanted to go through another pregnancy. She'd got used to her body being hers, and, as much as she'd never say it out loud, she already resented the baby for changing that.

"Fragile, you're certainly not, but precious, yes, always. I felt that way about you even before the pregnancy, so that hasn't changed anything."

She gritted her teeth. "It has. I can feel that you're different around me."

He threw up his hands, exasperated. "Is that any surprise?

"You have to trust me," she said. "It's as simple as that. Trust that I'm able to handle myself and that I know when to step back. Yes, this job might be more dangerous than most, but there are women in far more precarious situations than me who have babies."

"But they're not having *my* baby," he muttered and shook his head. "I'm walking on fucking eggshells, Erica. I can't say or do anything right. I know you're probably half crazy with hormones right—"

"You did not just play the hormone card on me?"

Maybe she was half crazy with hormones, but that didn't mean she wanted it pointed out to her, and especially not while she was at work and trying to do her job.

Shawn had always insisted it didn't matter to him if he didn't have a child of his own. He'd said that Poppy was enough for him. Erica had never fully believed him on that, and now it seemed his actions were proving him wrong. She didn't think he'd deliberately misled her, or lied, but perhaps he'd been kidding himself this whole time. He'd wanted them to be together so much that he'd convinced himself he could be happy without a family of his own. Her heart ached a little. Why wasn't *she* happy? He was getting everything he'd wanted, but she wasn't. It made her hate herself. Pregnant women should be happy and glowing, and wanting to nest and dreaming about their baby. Instead, she was moody and resentful, and, if she was truthful, downright terrified about going back to those days of no sleep and trying to juggle everything.

"Sorry, but—" he started.

She cut him off. "I can't do this right now. I'm your boss. We are at work, and you are being inappropriate. We've both got a job to do, so focus on that, okay?"

And with a shake of her head, she walked away.

Chapter Twenty-Three

F rances had spent the rest of the afternoon anxiously cleaning the house.

She'd left the letter sitting in the middle of the dining room table, and its presence was like a black hole in her world, threatening to pull her in.

She wished she could have torn it into a million pieces or taken it into the back garden and burned it in the fire pit, but it was evidence, and if she didn't keep hold of it, then she had nothing.

The click of the front door opening snatched her attention and sent her already racing heart rocketing.

The thought that it wasn't Matt coming into the house, but the person who'd posted the note, jumped into her head, and suddenly she found herself frozen, her breath locked in her chest.

"Frances?"

Matt's voice travelled through the house, and she was able to exhale again.

"I'm here," she called out.

She hurried through to greet him, snatching up the note from the table as she went.

He smiled when he saw her. "Hey, how was your—"

"Look at this." She slapped the letter against his chest.

All thoughts of being the perfect wife and showing him what he was missing had fled from her head. Now all she was thinking about was that someone had been to her home. They'd invaded her personal space. There were boundaries that shouldn't be crossed, and this was one of them, even if the person was just an innocent reader who wanted to pay her a compliment. Not that she thought that was the case.

He read the letter, his gaze flicking across the paper, and then glanced up and smiled. "That's nice."

She widened her eyes. "Nice? No, it's not nice. Someone put that through our letterbox. They came to our front door."

His forehead furrowed as he realised the implication of that. "Oh, right. Could it be someone you know then?"

"That doesn't make it any better if it is," she blurted. "If it was someone I know, why not sign their name? Why not just ring the doorbell like a normal person, so I can invite them in for a cup of tea? This is weird, and I don't like it, especially not after that young man was killed the other night."

"Oh, Frances, you can't possibly think the two things are connected?"

She threw up a hand. "They might be!"

He let out a breath and dragged his hand through his hair, clearly considering what to say next without her exploding. "Okay," he said levelly, "want do you want to do? You want to take this to the police? I don't think they're going to do much. It's not as though there's even a threatening word in it."

"The first thing I want us to do is order some security. I don't know why we haven't done it already. I want one of the doorbells with the camera in them, or even a security camera system that we can fix at the front and the back of the house, so everywhere is covered."

"You don't think that's a bit extreme?"

"No, I don't. Lots of people have them these days."

"The neighbours might not like it. They might feel like they're being spied on."

"Fuck the neighbours. You don't understand. It's different for you—you're a man. I'm here alone all day. I feel vulnerable, Matt."

Her eyes filled with tears again. Shit. When had she turned into such a crier?

"Hey, it's okay. We can get cameras. That's not a problem at all. We'll order them online. They'll be here within a day or two."

She sniffed. "And you'll install them?"

"Of course. It can't be that hard. I'm sure you can even link them up to your phone these days, so I can keep an eye on things when I'm not here. Will that make you feel better?"

"Yes, it will. Thank you." She bit her lower lip. "I'm sorry I'm such a headache. My brain doesn't know when to stop."

"I love your brain," he said, stepping closer to kiss her on the forehead. "Maybe it goes a bit over the top at times, but without it, you wouldn't be the creative, inspiring woman you are."

She warmed inside at his words. "Thank you. I just wish it would give me a break sometimes. It isn't easy living inside my head."

"It isn't always easy living outside of your head either," he admitted.

Her stomach twisted. "I know. I'm sorry."

She was terrified he'd leave her one day, that he'd just have enough and up and go. It wasn't as though they had children together. They didn't even share their finances, not really. They both had their own money, though they had a joint bank account that the bills all came out of. Matt put in a significant amount more than she did, as he earned so much more. She'd told herself it was the modern way, but now she worried that having everything so separate only meant that it would be easier to part.

He pulled her in for a hug, and she wrapped her arms around his waist and pressed her cheek to his chest. He was far from perfect, but she loved him, and she couldn't imagine her life without him in it.

If only she could make her fear of losing him override all her other fears.

Chapter Twenty-Four

E rica managed to get through the rest of the day without any more drama.

They were several days into a murder investigation, though, and she still didn't have any solid suspects. The search on the dropshipping premises was ongoing, but they hadn't found anything yet. Even if they did find what they were looking for, Luke Heale might be guilty of intent to supply, but that didn't make him a murderer. Even he wouldn't be stupid enough to bring that much attention to his business unnecessarily by pinning a man's body to the railings.

During the interview, which DI Julian Colgan had led, Heale had insisted there were no gangs or other competitors that he'd had a run-in with who might have left poor Taylor Quigley's body as a message. He denied that Taylor had ever bought drugs from him, but Erica still suspected the young man had been heading that way in order to score. Had someone followed him and seen their opportunity?

Or was Luke Heale lying to save his own arse?

The CCTV from Heale's business hadn't shown anything either. With the cameras pointed in the opposite direction of the murder, and that Heale only had them running during the hours he wasn't there—most likely to protect his own neck than anything else—they hadn't made any further progress.

It was incredibly frustrating.

If only they had Taylor's phone. She was sure it would have a wealth of information on it, but so far it hadn't turned up. She'd also heard from digital forensics, and though they'd managed to get into the laptop, it didn't look as though there was anything incriminating on it.

Hannah Rudd approached her desk. "Boss, I've been going through all the past orders from the dropshipping business and searched Taylor's name and address, and this came up."

She pushed a sheet of paper under Erica's nose. Several lines had been highlighted. "That's Taylor's address, right? It's not his full name, but it's enough to know those packages were intended for him."

Erica scanned the list. Taylor had been ordering items from Heale every other week for the past few months.

"How many pairs of socks does one person need?" she commented.

"Exactly. I bet it wasn't only socks that were in the package."

"Good work, Hannah. Did I tell you that I'm going to miss you?"

Hannah grinned. "By the sound of things, you're not going to be here to miss me."

"Oh, true, though only for a short while."

They had something linking Heale to Taylor now, but that still didn't mean Heale had been the one to kill him. She glanced over to where Shawn was at his desk, and her stomach clenched. There was a new kind of tension between them, and she wished she could make everything go back to how they had been. She got the feeling they weren't going to be playing happy families when they got home tonight.

Chapter Twenty-Five

The following morning, Erica was happy to get into the office.

As she'd anticipated, things had been tense at home, and it was easier to be surrounded by the team.

She felt a little bruised and achy from the fall yesterday, but it was nothing a couple of paracetamols couldn't sort out. Shawn hadn't mentioned it again, but she knew it was still playing on his mind.

They'd charged Heale with assaulting an officer, but as far as the drug charges went, they hadn't had anything to keep him. Much to her frustration, they still couldn't prove that Taylor's multiple orders had been anything other than socks, and it wasn't illegal to buy socks online. They still hadn't finished with their investigation, however. There was still a chance they'd come up with something that could nail Heale.

A commotion on the other side of the office caught her attention, and she lifted her head to see Shawn walking towards her desk.

"Boss, we've just had another emergency call come in. Middle-aged man found dead in his shed by his wife. Looks as though he's been killed with a nail gun."

"Killed with a nail gun?" she parroted. "Like in an accident, or deliberately?"

Shawn's expression was grim. "Definitely deliberately. He'd been nailed up to the inside of his shed door."

Erica was already on her feet, gathering her belongings. "Jesus."

"There's something else," Shawn said. "This murder might be connected to the railings case."

She paused. "Why do you say that?"

"Something has been carved into the victim's chest."

"Shit. Another N?"

"No. The responding officers say it's a circle."

She sucked in a breath. "Damn. What does it mean?"

"No idea. Is it a circle or is it an O? Is someone killing people in East London and branding them with letters?"

This was a disturbing turn of events. The killer had got a taste for death, and they seemed to be trying to send a message as well. Question was, what were they trying to say?

"Let's get over there."

Erica drove with the emergency lights flashing on the dashboard. They arrived in less than twenty minutes. She climbed out of the car and put on her jacket. The day was bright with a hint of a chill in the air. It would be autumn soon.

The house was a normal semi-detached property in a nice part of Haggerston, with a tidy front garden. No one could imagine the horror contained at the back of the house. Police tape looped across the front fence like a banner, and response vehicles were parked outside.

Erica and Shawn both pulled on protective clothing. They showed their IDs to an officer, who nodded his greeting, and then lifted the tape to allow them to duck underneath. A passageway around the right-hand side of the house allowed access to the rear garden.

Erica led the way.

Most of the activity was around the large shed in the corner of the garden. Scenes of Crime Officers, in protective white outerwear, and photographers carefully navigated around one another in the small space. Blocks had been placed down to prevent anyone from stepping in the blood or destroying possible footprints.

The shed door opened outward, and the man's body had been pinned to the inside of it.

The sergeant in charge of the scene jerked his chin at them as he saw them approaching. He was in his fifties with a bald head and a pair of glasses.

"Sergeant Philip Meeks," he introduced himself. "Thanks for coming so fast."

"DI Swift and DS Turner," she replied. "What have we got?"

"Sixty-seven-year-old Ian Grieve. Retired. His wife, Joyce, found him shortly after eleven when she was bringing him his morning cup of tea." He nodded down at where a mug had smashed on the paving stones. "The door was open, and she saw the body right away."

"Jesus, poor woman."

"They have two children, both grown. One of them lives in Reading and is on her way here now to be with her mother."

Erica stepped in closer to get a better view of the victim hanging from the inside of the shed door. Ian Grieve had been a skinny man, with an angular face and a full head of white hair. He wore a cream pair of cargo shorts and what had once been a light-blue polo shirt but was now dark red with blood. The front of the polo shirt had been slashed down the middle to expose his chest and the curve of the cuts marking his skin.

The wounds weren't what killed him, however. Neither were the multiple huge nails that had been punctured through the man's wrists, attaching him to the shed door. No, it was the nail punched into the side of Ian Grieve's temple that had most likely been the cause of death.

Like with Taylor Quigley, whoever did this must have been strong. Ian Grieve hadn't been a big man—probably the same weight Erica was, if not a little less in her current situation—but it still would have taken some strength to pin him up like this.

"Is the nail gun here?" she asked.

Meeks pointed inside the shed. "Yes, right there, on the surface."

It had been placed down on the work surface the victim used to do small woodwork jobs.

"With any luck, we'll get prints or DNA from it, but I've got the feeling the murderer is more methodical than that. I can't see him being stupid enough not to wear gloves."

Methodical. That was a good way of describing this killer. Everything seemed to be done deliberately, from the choosing of the victim, to the carving on the chest, to the way he'd been killed. It had been planned.

Did either of the victims have a connection? Did they know each other somehow? Or was their connection the identity of the man who'd killed them?

It was very rare for a murderer to choose his victims completely at random. So what was it connecting them?

Erica pictured Ian Grieve pottering around in here, getting jobs done that his wife had probably been nagging him about for ages. Had this small corner of the garden been his space? Like the front of the house, the garden was beautifully maintained, the borders of the lawn perfectly trimmed, the flowerbeds weed-free and blooming. How would his wife cope with him gone? Erica couldn't imagine her ever wanting to come out here again. How could she, without picturing her husband's final moments? She would probably never bring herself to enjoy the garden again.

Maybe they'd get lucky and be able to get a shoe print from one of the borders. How had the killer accessed the property? Had they come over one of the fences, or had they accessed the garden from the road, slipping around the side of the house in the same way they had only minutes before?

It was the middle of the day in the middle of the week. Most people, if they weren't retired or young parents, would be at work. It would be a quiet time. Had the killer taken advantage of that?

"This happened while the wife was inside the house?" she asked Meeks.

"That's right."

"And she didn't hear or see anything?"

"She says not." The sergeant pointed at a radio at the back of the shed. "She turned that off after she found him but said he'd been playing eighties rock music at full blast. Perhaps that drowned out any sounds he might have made."

Erica nodded. "Possibly, but I'd still expect there to be some kind of a struggle."

"Maybe he killed him first," Shawn suggested, "with the nail gun to the temple, and then pinned him up?"

Like a beetle to a display board.

Erica tried to play through events in her mind. "Then when he was nailed to the door, the killer cut his shirt and then carved the circle on his chest."

Sergeant Meeks sucked air over his teeth and shook his head. "The murderer is one cocky son of a bitch to do all of that with the wife in the house. Doesn't seem like he was in any rush or had a fear of getting caught."

Erica considered this. "Maybe he knew their routine—that she wouldn't come out until eleven with that cup of tea."

Shawn nodded. "If that was the case, then the killer had been watching them for some time to know their routine."

"We're going to need to interview all the neighbours, go door to door, find out if anyone saw or heard anything. See if any of them have CCTV."

Meeks nodded. "Already on it."

Erica stepped away from the shed. Like most of this area, the garden was overlooked. Living in London, finding a property that *wasn't* overlooked would be a miracle. Someone living in one of the properties would most likely have been aware of the couple's routine, but surely no one who lived in them had been stupid enough to kill a neighbour like this?

The kitchen was at the front of the house. The murderer could have watched from the street, waited until the wife appeared, and observed what she did. He could have stood at the side alley and seen Ian Grieve in the back garden. He didn't need to be in one of the neighbours' homes to learn their routine.

"Where's the victim's wife now?" Erica asked the sergeant.

"Inside the house with one of my officers. She's extremely distraught, understandably."

"I'm going to need to talk to her."

Erica stripped off her protective clothes and booties before she went into the house via the back door. Another uniformed police officer directed her through to the lounge.

Mrs Joyce Grieve sat on her floral sofa, shakily nursing a cup of tea which the young female officer sitting beside her must have made.

How terrible it must be, losing your husband at this time of life, and especially in such a violent way.

"Mrs Grieve, my name is DI Swift, and I'm the detective in charge of your husband's case. I realise this is a distressing time for you, but I wondered if I could have a quick word?"

"Yes, of course."

Erica perched on a chair opposite. It had the well-worn appearance of a chair that had been loved for many years. She wondered if this had been Mr Grieve's spot, the place where he'd sat every night to watch the television. Long marriages had a lot of habits ingrained in them, including everyone having their own seat, and she would put money on the place where Mrs Grieve was sitting now was where she'd sat every night, too.

"We've been married almost forty years," she said. "Together even longer. We met when I was twenty-two years old. I can't believe it's ended like this."

"I'm so sorry for your loss, Mrs Greive."

She wiped her eyes with a screwed-up tissue.

"Did your husband have any enemies?"

Mrs Grieve stared at her like she'd just offered her a trip to the moon. "Enemies? No, definitely not."

"No one he's fallen out with recently, no matter how trivial it might seem."

"He argues with the neighbours about them putting their bins out next to our front wall, but that's all, and they're in their eighties, so I highly doubt they'd have anything to do with something so terrible."

"What did he do as a job, before he retired?"

"He worked for the council."

"Could he have upset anyone there?"

"He retired five years ago. Surely if there had been a problem, it would have come up before now."

Erica nodded. "Yes, most likely, but I still want to explore every avenue. I understand you have two children?"

"Yes, well, they're adults now with families of their own. God, this is going to destroy them, and the grandchildren as well." Her chest hitched with another sob. "I don't want them to remember him like this."

"You'll remember him how you want to remember him," Erica said gently. "You'll keep his memory alive."

Joyce wiped her eyes again. "Thank you. I hope so."

Chapter Twenty-Six

F rances sat at her computer, staring at the manuscript she was supposed to be working on. All the comments and highlighted areas made her want to groan, but she knew it would be a better book when she was done. Blaire could be a real taskmaster when he wanted to be, but she did appreciate him.

The shrill ring of her doorbell cut through the house, and she jumped at the sound, clutching her hand to her chest. That was the trouble when she was lost in work—she had no awareness of anything going on around her, and everything made her jump.

Crazily, her thoughts went to the person who'd put the note through her door. What if it was the one and same, only now she was going to come face to face with them?

No, she was being paranoid. It was more likely just a delivery driver with a package. She needed to stop leaping to the worst conclusions all the time.

Frances pushed back her chair and got to her feet. She went to the front door and paused. There was patterned glass in the door, and the distorted shape of a figure stood beyond.

She opened the door to find her brother-in-law standing on the doorstep.

He was so similar to his brother, except a shorter, stockier version.

Frances couldn't act pleased to see him. "What are you doing here, Pete?"

He peered over her shoulder. "Looking for Matt. Is he in?"

"No, he's at work."

Why would he think Matt would be here? Pete knew what long hours Matt worked. Why hadn't he gone to the office, or at least phoned or texted him and asked where he was? Something about this whole encounter was putting her teeth on edge. All her nerve endings had suddenly come alight, and her fight-or-flight instinct had stepped up a notch.

"Oh right," Pete said. "Time for a cup of tea?"

To her shock, he pushed past her and headed straight for the kitchen.

She followed him through. "Umm, I'm in the middle of work, actually. I don't really have time to stop for a cup of tea."

"Don't be daft." He was already at the kettle, filling it with fresh water and flicking the switch. "Everyone's got time for a cuppa. I won't keep you long."

He opened her cupboards, searching for the mugs. The kettle fizzed and then roiled and clicked off.

"Seriously, Pete, what are you doing here?"

"Oh, Matt left his bank card at mine." Pete fished into his back pocket of his jeans to produce the green slip of plastic. "I didn't want him to worry and figured he'd probably need it, so I thought I'd return it."

He placed it on the kitchen counter.

"Right. Thanks."

She was still thrown by his presence. Could he have taken Matt's bank card so he had an excuse to come over here? Why would he do that? She watched him make two cups of tea and then he carried one over to her and set it down on the table in front of her. He took a seat and pulled his own mug into his hands as though to keep them warm.

"So, how are the books going?" he asked. "Still writing?"

"Of course. It's my job. If I don't write, I don't pay my bills."

He scoffed at that. "Well, my brother would pay them for you, wouldn't he? He probably does already."

Matt *did* pay the larger sum of their mortgage and bills, but that was understandable since he earned a lot more money. He'd never once complained about it—at least not to her. Had he been moaning at his brother over a couple of pints, though? She hoped not. Their finances were none of Pete's business.

"I always warn him about you."

She jerked back in shock. "What?"

He chuckled. "All these murder books you write. I bet that kind of research means you'd know exactly what to do if you wanted to get rid of a husband and take all his money."

Was he being serious, or was this his way of being funny?

Feeling awkward and unsure, she gave a small laugh and decided to fight fire with fire. "Or if I wanted to get rid of my husband's brother," she said, trying to keep her tone light.

Something in his eyes darkened. "Matt tells me you've got a lot of mental health issues."

Her jaw dropped. "He what?"

Pete twirled his fingers beside his head. "Yeah, that you convince yourself you're sick all the time, even though you're fine. Sounds a bit batshit crazy to me."

"He shouldn't be discussing anything to do with my health with you."

She ground her molars. How dare Matt talk to Pete about her. But then she reined herself back in. Her issues couldn't be easy for Matt to deal with. He needed someone to talk to, didn't he? Even so, she'd have preferred he pay for a therapist rather than talk to Pete. It was as though Pete had gone to war on her, and her husband had been the one to provide him with the ammunition.

Her hands trembled in anger. It was all she could do to stop herself picking up the scalding hot cup of tea and throwing it in his face. For one insane moment, she pictured herself doing just that, his skin turning red while he clutched his hands to his face.

Pete wasn't finished. "You're holding him back, you know that, don't you? He has to cater to all your crazy ideas, day in, day out, when he could be having fun. You've aged him."

"Jesus Christ, no I haven't. He's just grown up, that's all. Maybe you could do with taking a leaf out of his book."

"And marry someone like you? No thanks. That sounds like a prison sentence to me."

"Matt is with me because he loves me."

Pete snorted. "So he says, whatever the hell that even means."

Somehow, she managed to keep her cool. "I feel sad for you, to be honest, if you don't understand what love means. I also think it's time for you to leave."

"I haven't finished my tea."

"And I don't care. Thank you for returning Matt's bank card. I'll let him know you stopped by."

She gestured towards the door.

He got to his feet. "Fine. I've got better things to do with my time than hang around here anyway."

"Believe me, I've got better things to do than argue with you, too."

He left the mug sitting on the table and stormed out towards the door. Without another word, he marched out of the house, and she slammed the door shut behind him. She pressed her back to it, shaking all over, her heart crashing against her ribs. That son of a bitch. Who the hell did he think he was, coming into her house and saying all that shit to her.

But it was all true, a poisonous little voice whispered in her head. *He's just looking out for his brother.*

She'd never had siblings, so she had no idea what it was like to have a brother or sister. Would she be as protective if she had a sister who she felt was with the wrong man? Pete had still well overstepped the mark, though. It wasn't as though Matt was in some kind of violent or abusive relationship. Maybe it wasn't perfect, but what was?

Should she tell Matt what his brother had said? The last thing she wanted was to come between the two of them. If she did that, she'd only be proving Pete right. But the bloke was such a fucking arsehole, didn't Matt deserve to know what sort of things he was saying to her? Deep down, though, she had the feeling Matt already knew. She doubted Pete held back when they were together, especially after they'd had a few drinks.

Anger roiled and churned inside her, but mixed in was panic. If she told Matt, he might take his brother's side. That was her biggest fear. He might decide Pete was completely right and that he'd be better off without her.

Then what would she do?

Chapter Twenty-Seven

When she got back to the office, Erica went to see DCI Gibbs.

"Sir, I'm going to need more resources. With this latest development, we're all just stretched too thin."

"I understand. I'll bring some more bodies in. Are these two murders connected?"

"I believe so. Even though the ways they were killed was different, we can't ignore the circle carved into the victim's chest. That's a piece of information we held back from the public, so there's little chance of it being a copycat."

"But there's nothing connecting the two victims?" he checked.

"Not that we've found so far. On paper, they're about as different as two people can get, other than that they're both male."

"And how are you feeling after yesterday? No lasting damage?"

"I'm fine, sir, honestly. A bit achy, but that's all. No harm done."

"Shame we didn't have anything else to pin on the arsehole," Gibbs said.

"We still might, with the search of the premises not yet complete, but with this new murder..." She blew out a breath. "Well, it's probably not going to take priority now."

They only had a certain number of people, and if they were spread too thin, they were bound to miss something. They were doing the best they could with the resources they had.

Erica left the office and called a briefing to fill the team in on this new development. She knew they were all going to be overwhelmed, but now they needed to tie in what information they had from Taylor Quigley's case to this one.

Her phone rang. It was Sergeant Philip Meeks.

"I don't know if it's anything," he said, "but one of my officers spoke to a neighbour who saw someone acting suspiciously last night. Said a man in a black hoodie, with it pulled up to cover his face, was lurking on the street."

"Was time was this?"

"Around eleven last night. They were coming home from work. The figure had their head down and seemed to be looking for something, but when the neighbour turned into the road, they took off."

"They were on foot?" she asked.

"That's right."

"Any luck with security cameras?"

"Not yet," he replied. "We're still working on it."

Without any images, knowing someone in a black hoodie was hanging around the area wouldn't be much use to them.

"Okay. Keep me updated."

She ended the call and then filled Shawn in on what she'd been told.

"Do you think it's anything?" he said.

She thought about it. "Could have been our guy scoping out the place? Or might have been nothing. My gut tells me that he'd have been doing it in the daytime if he'd know exactly what time Mrs Grieve came out with a cup of tea."

He rubbed his finger across his lips. "There's one other possibility we haven't considered."

"Which is?"

"That the killer was known to the Grieves. They didn't know their routine because they were spying on them. Perhaps they just knew because they'd been here before, or simply because either Mr or Mrs Grieve told them."

She nodded slowly. "That's a very good point. What about Taylor Quigley, though? Mrs Grieve didn't recognise the name, though she was aware of the murder. She'd seen it on the news. Is there a connection between the two men? On paper, they couldn't be more different. Two different generations. One married, the other single. One liked to garden, while the other enjoyed partying. I can't see what could possibly be connecting them."

He cocked his head. "Apart from the fact they were both murdered and had a letter carved into their chests."

She picked up a pen and wrote two letters down on a notepad. "N and O. What are they saying no to? Is the killer trying to tell us that they're saying no to something? Is this a protest of some kind?"

It wouldn't be the first time someone had been murdered for a cause.

"Or they're someone's initials?" he suggested.

Erica wished they knew something for certain. At the moment, it all felt like guesswork, and she needed proof.

Chapter Twenty-Eight

Frances stared at her phone screen, her eyes wide. Her stomach dropped, and she grew short of breath, as though her lungs had forgotten how to breathe. The room around her seemed to spin, and she clutched the table beside her, praying it would keep her upright.

No, this couldn't be happening.

She read the article again, hoping that she'd misread it somehow. A pressure built inside her temples, and she placed her fingers against the point where it hurt the worst, hoping to alleviate it. What if she was going to have a brain haemorrhage? What if all the stress was too much, and her blood pressure was too high, and something inside her was going to fatally explode?

She half bent, forcing herself to take deep breaths. She didn't want to believe it, but it was there in black and white. There had been a second murder.

The kitchen door opened, and Matt walked in. Upon finding her bent over, gasping for breath, he drew up short.

"You okay?"

"Look at this!" Frances cried, straightening up and shoving her phone at her husband. "A man has been killed with a nail gun. A gruesome discovery, the reporters are saying. Died in his shed, nailed to the goddamn door."

He frowned down at the phone. "That's terrible, but I don't understand why you're getting so worked up."

"If you ever bothered to read one of my books, then you'd know. This is exactly how I kill one of my victims in *Bound for Slaughter*. You still think it's a coincidence after the last one?"

He stared at her. "Yes, of course I think it's a coincidence. I mean, how many ways are there to kill a person?"

"Plenty," she insisted. "Trust me, I've done my research."

"But you don't know these people. Why the hell would someone do such a thing? I think you're seeing connections where there aren't any."

"What are you talking about? Of course there are connections. I was worried at the first one, and now there's been a second. I know it's crazy, but what if someone is copying the murders from my books?" She thought of something else. "Oh my God, I got that letter yesterday, too. What if it was from the killer? What if they know where I live and I'll be next?"

"Now you really are blowing things out of proportion. Someone sent you a perfectly lovely note saying how much they admire your books—"

"Admire them enough to act out the murders?"

He shook his head. "You're crazy."

Her eyes swam with tears. Was she crazy? She knew she let her thoughts and paranoia get away from her sometimes. She had a fear of death, and somehow she'd managed to create a career where all she did was immerse herself in it. Why couldn't she have written romance, or sci-fi, or historical? Why was she so drawn to it? It was as though by facing the most horrific ways of dying that she could think of, it would shield her from it happening to her.

Now these murders were far too close for comfort.

"I'm going to speak to the detective in charge of the case. Maybe she'll think I'm crazy, too, but at least I'll have said my piece. What if there's another murder, and I could have said or done something to prevent it but instead I kept my mouth shut because I was worried about embarrassing myself?"

He shook his head. "Do what you want, Frances. You always do."

Her mouth fell open. "What's that supposed to mean?"

"You never pay any attention to anything I have to say. You ask my opinion on things and then never take my advice. You worry all the time about your health, even though you've barely had anything more serious than a headache, and it doesn't matter how many times I reassure you that you're fine, you never take any notice. I'm not even sure why I bother speaking anymore."

Frances cringed. "I'm sorry. I can't help it."

"You don't even try."

"Matt..." She'd said his name but had no idea what she was going to say after. What was she supposed to do? Accept what he'd said in order to keep the peace and potentially allow someone else to be murdered? His pride wasn't worth that price.

She didn't know any details about the murders—the police didn't release those kinds of details so they were able to distinguish time-wasters from people with real information—but she was fairly sure she could describe the scene the police had found. She could picture it in her mind's eye; the position of the body, the number of nails used, even the approximate age and description of the victim.

"How many books have you written?" Matt suddenly asked.

She couldn't see where he was going with this. "Twelve—eleven that are published. Why?"

"How many people are murdered in all those pages?"

She thew up her hands. "I don't know. At least a couple of people in each book, sometimes more."

"So you could have written at least twenty-five murders, maybe more. How many different ways are there to kill a person? I assume you like to be inventive in the ways that people die, so isn't it possible that you've written pretty much every possible murder?"

"You're saying that no matter how someone is killed, I'm going to find some connection to a murder in one of my books?"

He seemed pleased with himself. "Exactly."

"No. I don't believe that."

But even so, his words had been enough to thread doubt into her mind. Was she just reading something into nothing? She had a history of paranoia. Was she losing her mind?

A tear slipped down her cheek, and she wiped it away with the heel of her hand.

"Hey, it's okay," he said, pulling her into a hug. "It's part of your job to have an overactive imagination."

She let him hug her, but at the same time she wanted to say that she wasn't imagining that people were being murdered. That was very real. Perhaps they weren't connected to her books, but it was still scary. The victims hadn't been found very far from here—different boroughs, yes, but still not far away. What if someone decided to hurt them next?

She'd made up her mind. She'd tell the detective in charge of the case about her suspicions. If the detective thought there was nothing in it, then she'd force herself to put all this to the back of her mind and not read any more of the news reports.

Chapter Twenty-Nine

It was late, and it had been a long day. Erica was looking forward to getting home and collapsing on the sofa. She wished they'd made more progress, but sometimes it was better to let it go for the day and start again the following morning with a fresh head. She knew the rest of the team were tired, too. It had been an intense week so far, and there weren't any signs that things would crack in the case anytime soon.

She stepped out of the building and headed to her car.

"DI Swift?"

A pretty blonde woman stood in the car park. She seemed anxious, nervous, her mouth pinched and lines between her brows. She had a handbag on her shoulder, and she clutched the strap with the opposite arm, creating a subconscious shield across her chest. Her knuckles were white. Dark shadows bruised her eyes, like she hadn't been sleeping.

"Yes, can I help you?"

"Honestly, I'm not sure. My name is Frances Gilchrist." The woman hesitated, watching Erica's face as though she expected Erica to recognise her. When it was clear she didn't, she carried on. "I'm a writer—an author. I write crime fiction."

Erica tried not to show how baffled she was about why this young woman had approached her. Was this some kind of new promotion method? If so, it was terrible. Or maybe she was hoping to interview Erica for research reasons. If so, there was no way Erica had time for anything like that.

"I'm sorry, Miss Gilchrist, but I'm still not sure—"

"Mrs," the other woman corrected her. "But call me Frances, please."

"Frances," Erica repeated. "I'm not completely sure why you needed to speak to me."

Frances's cheeks turned pink. "No, I'm sorry. I'm not making myself very clear, am I. Honestly, I feel a bit stupid coming to talk to you, but I couldn't put it off any longer. I figured if I told you, and you thought there was nothing in it, then it would at least put my mind at rest."

Frances glanced furtively from side to side and lowered her voice to a near hiss. "It's about the murders of those two men."

Erica hadn't been expecting that. "Oh, right. I guess we'd better go inside. Come this way."

She tried not to think about how she was supposed to be picking Poppy up from Natasha's in thirty minutes. She pinged a quick text off to Shawn to see if he could do it.

She got a few raised eyebrows from colleagues at her reappearance, and she offered them small smiles in return. She led the young woman through to one of the interview rooms, checking it was empty, and then punched in the code to let them both inside.

"We'll have some privacy in here," Erica said, gesturing to one of the chairs for Frances to sit down.

"Thank you."

Frances perched on one of the chairs, her handbag clutched in her lap.

"Can I get you a coffee or water, or anything?"

Frances shook her head. "No, thank you. I won't keep you for long."

Erica couldn't imagine she was here to confess to two brutal murders, but was it possible she knew the person who had, or at least had suspicions about their guilt?

"What was it you needed to tell me, Frances?"

"I told you I write crime books, right? Well, the two murders that have happened recently are from my books?"

Erica blinked. "I'm sorry."

"I describe them in my books. The man found on the railings is from *A Perfect Death*, and the man with the nail gun in his shed is from *Bound for Slaughter*." She reached into her bag and pulled out two paperbacks. Coloured slips protruded from within the pages. "I've highlighted and marked the paragraphs so you didn't need to read the whole thing. I'm not sure the rest of the books are relevant, but I don't know, maybe they are."

Was this woman a time-waster? Someone desperate for attention? Was this some kind of publicity stunt? Erica didn't know what to think.

She reached across the table and took the two paperbacks. There was nothing particularly eye-catching about the covers—both showed women with their backs to the covers in an urban location. She flipped to the front and checked the publication dates. Both had been published within the last couple of years.

She read one of the highlighted paragraphs. "—the pointed spike glistened, slick with the man's blood. Small white pieces of bone and brain caught in the pale moonlight. The man wasn't quite yet dead, his limbs trembling like a person with palsy. His gaze locked, unseeing, on the figure who'd just ended his life—" Erica paused. "Gruesome."

Frances nodded, the action small and tight. "People do say that. They don't expect it from me."

"I can see why not."

"Read the next one," Frances encouraged.

Erica placed the first paperback down on the table and picked up the second one. Like with the first, the chapter had been marked out, and she easily flicked through pages until she reached it.

"—nails punctured his palms, and through his feet, pinning him to the wood behind. Blood trickled from the wounds, creating a trail down his skin and onto the floor."

"Do you see what I mean?" Frances said, leaning forwards slightly. "I've described the murders, haven't I? Except I wrote those scenes several years ago, and the murders have only just happened."

Erica pressed her lips together. "What are you suggesting? That someone is copying the murders from your books?"

"Is it that far-fetched?" There was a strange kind of hope in the author's tone.

"Who were the killers?" Erica asked.

"Sorry?"

"In the books," she prompted. "Who was responsible for killing the two victims in your books."

"Um..." Frances thought for a moment.

"You don't know?"

"I wrote them a long time ago. I've written lots of books since then. Once I've finished writing, the plots just go straight out of my head." She paused again and then said, "Oh, yes, I remember now. In *Bound for Slaughter* it was a disgruntled employee who killed his boss's boss after they'd been made to announce redundancies which ruined his life. He lost his home, and his wife left him, so he decided to take out his anger on the man who was the catalyst to it all."

"And for *A Perfect Death*?"

Frances thought again. "That was a jealous lover who was killing anyone who shared an appearance with the man who his wife had an affair with."

Erica raised an eyebrow. "Really?"

"People have killed each other over less."

She was probably right about that, and anyway, this was fiction. It didn't need to be too realistic—it was created for entertainment, not to mirror real life. Except, on this occasion, had it mirrored real life? No, it was just a coincidence, surely? While the paragraphs certainly seemed to be the same as the crimes she was investigating, she struggled to believe someone would kill people on the basis of some books. Murders were normally down to three things: jealousy, money, or revenge.

"There's something else," Frances said. "I feel like someone has been watching me. It's mainly just an instinct, a feeling, but there's also been this." She reached back into her handbag and pulled out a slip of paper.

She slid it across the table, and Erica picked it up. She unfolded it and read the contents.

"The letter was put through my letterbox. They came to my house."

"I see."

Erica read the note. There was nothing in it that seemed threatening at all, though she could understand that the invasion of privacy would make Frances uncomfortable.

"Can you leave this with me?" She nodded down at the letter. "Has anyone else handled it?"

"My husband, Matt. No one else."

"I'll get it dusted for prints and checked for DNA, see if it matches anything at our crime scenes. Other than that, I'm not sure where else to go with this. I assume you don't have a video doorbell, or you would have already checked if you'd caught someone on camera?"

"No, I haven't, but we've got one on order. It should arrive any day now. My husband has promised to install it."

"They can be useful," Erica said.

Erica had no idea what else she could do with this information. It wasn't as though there was much else they could use to catch the killer. Would there be more murders? Would the next one also be from one of Frances Gilchrist's books? Or was this just a coincidence? It wasn't as though they could even use the books to predict the murders. How many had she written?

It occurred to Erica that there was a possibility Frances herself could be involved. What about the husband? She'd get a background check done on both.

She picked the books back up. "Mind if I keep hold of these?"

"Of course not. I meant for you to keep them."

"In which case," Erica picked her pen up and then slid the two books and the pen back over to Frances, "do you mind signing them for me?"

Frances seemed a little flustered at the question. "Oh, no, I don't mind."

Her hand was shaking as she opened to the title page of the book and quickly scribbled her name. She repeated the process in the second book and then handed them back to Erica.

Erica thought of something. "Do you always kill men off in your books?"

"Not always, no."

"But each of the murders that have been copied, it's been men who are killed. Aren't women normally the victims in books?"

Frances folded her hands and glanced down. "Women are normally the victims, full stop. Maybe that's why I prefer writing male victims. Give the women a break."

"Fair enough."

Was Frances a man-hater? She was married, wasn't she? How did she feel about her husband?

"Where were you when the murders occurred?"

Frances seemed to think. "The first one? I was with my husband all night. As for the second...it happened during the day, didn't it? In which case, I was home, alone, except for when my brother-in-law came over for a cup of tea."

Something Erica couldn't read flickered across the author's face.

"Did you mention the similarities between your books and the murders to your publisher?" Erica questioned.

"I may have mentioned something casually to my editor, Blaire, but I thought I was overthinking it at that stage. I had my suspicions but when I mentioned it to my husband, he thought I was crazy." She twirled a hand in the air beside her head. "I've had some...issues. I have health anxiety. It's a type of OCD. It means I obsess about getting sick. I lost my parents very suddenly within a year of each other, and I think it started shortly after that. I guess the reason I'm telling you is so you understand that it means I have a habit of blowing things up in my head. Seeing catastrophe where there isn't one. It's why my husband wasn't so quick to believe me. Well, that and the whole thing sounding insane."

So she had mental health issues. Did that make any difference? It was as though half the population struggled with something or another—which was hardly surprising in society these days.

"Did you know either of the victims?" Erica asked.

"No, I don't think so."

"Could there be any connections you have with either of them?"

"Not that I know of. The only thing that links me is that I'm the one who created their murders, at least in my imagination. I can't help blaming myself. If I'd never written those scenes, would those poor people still be alive?"

Erica offered her a rueful smile. "You can't blame yourself for other people's actions. Besides, there is a good chance these murders have nothing to do with your books. I admit, it's a very bizarre coincidence, but right now, there's no evidence."

Frances opened her mouth and then closed it again. "I see. So, what now?"

"I'm not sure what to think. I'll admit, it's one hell of a coincidence. Can you leave it with me?" Erica handed her one of her cards. "But get in touch if you think of anything else."

"Yes, of course." Frances got to her feet and slipped the card into her handbag. She nodded down at the books. "I hope you enjoy them."

Chapter Thirty

I *hope you enjoy them?*

Frances felt like smacking herself in the forehead.

What the hell had she said that for? It wasn't as though she'd been at a book signing. She'd handed those books over to the detective as part of a murder inquiry. The detective wasn't reading them for fun.

Sometimes, Frances wished the ground would open up and swallow her.

Her phone buzzed, and she checked the screen. It was a message from Matt asking where she was. Should she tell him that she'd spoken to the police? What would he say? The whole thing seemed to only make him angry. Why was that? He was normally so supportive of her, but it was as though he'd finally run out of patience.

She quickly typed out a reply.

<On my way home now. See you soon. Xx>

She'd promised herself that once she'd told her suspicions to the police, she'd let it drop, but she had the feeling that was going to be easier said than done. What more was she supposed to do? If the police didn't think there was anything in it, then she needed to leave it be.

Unfortunately, Frances didn't have the kind of brain that liked to leave things be. Instead of obsessing about her health, now she was obsessing about the killer.

The security cameras for the house were due to arrive tomorrow morning. Matthew had promised he'd install them—one for the front, and one for back. She just hoped she wouldn't end up obsessing over the footage. She could link it to her phone so she'd be able to watch the front and rear of her property whenever she liked.

It would bring her some reassurance, though. If someone was sneaking onto her property, she'd catch them on camera.

Frances reached her car, unlocked it, and climbed behind the wheel. Still lost in thought, she just sat there, unable to function enough to get the car moving.

From the building she'd just been inside, she spotted DI Swift leaving again and crossing the car park to her own car.

Had the detective taken her seriously? She thought so, but then had the detective also implied that Frances might be connected to the murders? That maybe her and her husband had something to do with them?

That was ridiculous.

No, she just needed to leave it now. Let the police do their jobs. There was nothing more she could do.

Chapter Thirty-One

E rica lay in bed later, staring at the darkened ceiling, unable to sleep. Shawn lay beside her, but she could tell he wasn't asleep either. She'd already told him all about the strange meeting she'd had with the author.

She was grateful to be able to run it all past him.

"It couldn't be some crazy publicity stunt, could it?" she said into the dark.

"What, they're actually murdering people to make the books sell better?"

Erica thought about it. "I'm not sure a lifetime in prison is worth hitting a bestseller list."

"You never know, some authors might be happy to make that exchange."

She could hear the grin in his tone.

"Unlikely, but I'll definitely look into them both further." She sighed and threw up her hands. "I just don't know what to do with this. Is it real? Or just a coincidence? And, if it is real, how the hell do we use it?"

"Someone connected to the author?" he suggested. "A crazed fan, perhaps?"

"A deranged fan, if that's really the case. And if it is the case, then we have to consider that the author herself might also be in danger. She seemed extremely nervous and anxious when she came to me."

He twisted to face her and pillowed his palm under his cheek. "Can you blame her? I'd be exactly the same if I thought someone out there was so obsessed with something I'd written that they were actually murdering people because of it. I imagine, if she really believes this, there's some guilt attached as well. If she hadn't written those words, then those people would still be alive."

Erica sighed. "I can't believe we're actually considering this. It's crazy."

They lay in silence for a few moments, both lost in thought.

"I asked her to sign the books," Erica said.

"Why?"

"I wanted to see what her reaction would be. If she'd kind of blow up, all proud, like."

"Did she?"

"No, the opposite. It seemed to embarrass her." Erica turned to her side to face him. "I think I asked so I could see if she got off on the idea of fame and being recognised."

"You don't think she has anything to do with this, do you?"

"I'm fairly sure it's just a coincidence," she said. "But the author seemed convinced."

"Maybe her and her husband are working on it together."

She gave a small laugh. "She writes the murders, and he reenacts them for her."

He grinned at her. "Your pillow talk is always the best, did I ever tell you that?"

"Probably," she admitted. She let out a sigh. "I'm worried that if she's right, there's going to be another murder. Not only that, she could be in danger as well."

"I guess this is why authors have pen names."

"True, though I can't really see the point if you're going to do live events like readings and signings. People are going to see you then. They'll take photographs. In this day and age, if someone wants to find out your identity, then they will."

"Everyone's an investigator, huh?" Shawn said.

"The only thing she didn't mention was the letters carved into the men's chests. Those weren't in her books, and she didn't seem to know about them either."

Erica didn't have much time for reading these days. She used to all the time when she'd been younger—pre-Poppy, and when she used to take holidays in the sun. Then, there had been nothing she enjoyed more than lying on the beach or by the pool with a good paperback. She couldn't remember the last time she'd even picked up a book, and the realisation shamed her a little.

"Do you think she's a time-waster?" Shawn asked. "Someone trying to get attention?"

"She didn't come across that way, but it's a possibility."

"You don't really believe they're murdering people as a publicity stunt?"

Erica gave a small laugh. "Well, maybe not the murdering part, but perhaps claiming they're connected. It would certainly get some eyes on her books. I checked her out, and she's got a new one releasing in a few months. She didn't seem the type, but who knows."

She stifled a wide yawn behind her hand.

"Enough of work talk," Shawn said. "You need some sleep."

He was right. It was going to be another full-on day tomorrow.

Chapter Thirty-Two

The briefing room was fuller than normal.

With two murders to investigate now, their numbers had swelled.

They had hours of CCTV footage from the local area to meticulously review. Possible witnesses to question. Reports from SOCO to go through, as well as photographs from the scene, and the pathologist's report.

Erica made sure everyone knew what their actions were. She was about to return to her desk when her stomach felt a little loose, and she detoured to the bathroom instead.

She went into one of the stalls to relieve herself, but the moment she pulled down her underwear, her stomach dropped.

Her knickers were red with blood.

Suddenly it was like there were insects buzzing in her ears. Adrenaline shot through her veins, and the small bathroom stall seemed to close in around her. She put out her hand to steady herself against the wall.

Oh God, no. Not this.

Women bled during pregnancy, didn't they? It was common. It didn't mean the worst. But she didn't think they meant this kind of bleeding. They meant spotting, where this was more like clots.

Her eyes filled with tears, and she put her face in her hands. What the fuck was she supposed to do now? Her mind went in a million different directions. What about Shawn? What about Poppy? They were both going to be crushed. But also, stupidly, she questioned if she had time to go to the hospital. She was in the middle of this case. There was a madman out there murdering innocent people. She didn't have time for this.

Her stomach cramped, and she hunched over. Tears spilled from her eyes, and she wiped them away with her hand.

This could have happened at any time. Hadn't she been warned that at her age, she was a higher risk pregnancy? Somehow, she hadn't believed it was going to happen, though. She'd carried Poppy with no issues, and she'd thought this one would be the same.

She didn't want to worry anyone. It could be nothing. She still wanted to believe that.

She grabbed some more tissue paper for her underwear. She sniffed and blinked fast a few times, trying to clear her eyes. She didn't want anyone to notice that she'd been crying.

She sorted herself out best she could and left the bathroom.

Erica walked quickly through the office, keeping her head down, allowing her hair to fall over her face in the hope of disguising her blotchy skin. She picked up her handbag and jacket from her desk.

Shawn wasn't anywhere to be seen, and she found herself feeling relieved about that. She needed him to stay at the office, and if he knew something was wrong, he'd insist on coming with her.

"I have to go out," she called over to Hannah. "Hold the fort for me, okay?"

"Everything okay?" Hannah asked.

But Erica just kept going and didn't answer. She'd have her phone if anyone needed her. She trusted her team. They could manage.

She was shaky and upset, but she was okay to drive. The hospital wasn't far away, but the traffic was its usual slow crawl. Another cramp wrung through her, and she hung on tight to the steering wheel and tried not to cry.

It felt like the longest drive of her life, and then when she did finally arrive, she couldn't find anywhere to park. Tears trembled in her eyes, wobbling her vision. She tried her best to remain calm, knowing that it wouldn't help anything if she lost control.

Finally, someone pulled out of a space in front of her, and she almost sobbed in relief. She slotted the car into the spot, used her phone to pay for the parking, and then made her way into the hospital. She'd attended the maternity unit before, so knew which way to go.

She found the reception desk, and the nurse sitting there smiled up at her. "Can I help?"

Erica did her best to keep her voice level, though a tremor of emotion ran through her words. "My name is Erica Swift. I think I'm having a miscarriage. I'm bleeding heavily, and there are clots."

"How far along are you?"

"Seventeen weeks."

The nurse gave her a small smile of sympathy. "Okay, take a seat over there." She nodded to the plastic bank of chairs which contained women with huge, swollen bellies, and their families. "I'll try to get someone to look at you as soon as possible."

Erica made it over to one of the chairs before pain shot through her and she let out a groan. Sweat coated her forehead, her hair clinging to her skin.

She tried not to think about all the baby books that described what the baby was like at this stage. It hurt too much to even think she was losing an actual baby.

"Erica?" A female doctor approached. "I'm Doctor Eastman. Would you like to come with me, and we'll get you checked over."

Erica nodded and got back to her feet.

The doctor went through a number of questions and then took her into a private room that had an ultrasound machine. "I'm sorry, this will be cold."

"It's okay."

She went through the routine of having the cold gel applied, and then the wand pressed low on her stomach. The doctor stared at the screen. Erica couldn't even look. She already knew, deep down, what the doctor was going to say.

"I'm so sorry, but I'm afraid I can't find a heartbeat."

Erica gulped a sob and nodded. She couldn't speak. She'd expected to hear that news, but it still came as a shock. There was no going back from this now. It was over.

"Is there anyone we can call to be with you?"

She shook her head. Natasha was watching Poppy after school that day, and Shawn would be needed at work. The team couldn't afford to have both of them absent.

She'd get through this. Just like she got through everything.

"Are you sure?" the doctor questioned.

"Yes, I'll be okay."

The nurse talked her through her options, including waiting for her body to deal with things naturally.

"I don't want that. I just want this to be over."

"I understand. Do you want to go home first, or else I've got a cancelled surgery spot, if you want it? You'll need to sign some forms for the doctor to conduct the surgery."

"Yes, that's fine."

She stared at the painted white ceiling with the harsh lights. Time went by, but she was lost in thought, withdrawn. She was barely aware of the doctors and nurses around her, the forms she signed, the sedative she was given. Thankfully, most of it was a blank after that.

She came back around in a different hospital room. Her belongings in the small cabinet beside her. A nurse smiling down at her.

"Is it over? I want to go home."

"Yes." The nurse ran her through some aftercare. "You can't go home just yet. You lost a considerable amount of blood. We need to keep you in overnight for observations."

All she could think of was Shawn and Poppy. They were both going to be devastated. She didn't want to tell them, but she had no choice. She curled up on her side, feeling empty, physically and emotionally.

She must have dozed. When she woke again, it was to her phone ringing. Shit. How much time had passed? People were going to wonder what had happened to her. She reached for her bag, which contained her phone, and put her hand on it.

Shawn's name was on screen. She swiped to answer.

"Hi."

"Erica, where are you?"

"Shawn, I'm sorry, but I'm in hospital."

His tone was immediately alarmed. "What? Why? Is everything all right?"

"No, it's not. I lost the baby."

"Oh God. I'm on my way."

He ended the call, and she dropped her phone onto the bed beside her and curled back up again. She closed her eyes. The medication they'd given her was making it hard to stay awake, and she drifted off. When she opened her eyes again, Shawn was at her bedside.

Seeing him was hard. She felt as though she'd failed him, had let him down, and she couldn't stand seeing the pain in his eyes. It was as though she'd been the one to cause it, which, she guessed she had been. Should she have gone to get checked out after she'd fallen? Would anything be different if she had? The sensible part of her knew that if damage had been done then, the pregnancy was too early for the doctors to have done anything, but the heartbroken part of her blamed herself.

"Jesus, Erica. I'm so sorry. Are you okay?" He took her hand, his grip warm and firm.

She couldn't answer that. All she could manage was a shrug.

"You should have called me the minute you realised something was wrong."

"I didn't know for sure. I didn't want to worry you if it was nothing."

"But it wasn't nothing, was it?" He shook his head. "What happened?"

She turned her face away. "I don't know. It's just one of those things. We were warned this was a high-risk pregnancy."

He sat and lowered his forehead to press it to her palm. "I know, but still..." He hitched a breath. "Did you tell the doctors about what happened? About how that arsehole pushed you over?"

"What would be the point?"

"We could charge him with the murder of our baby!"

She closed her eyes. "Shawn..."

There was no way they could ever prove that in court. Yes, she'd been pushed, but this might have still happened even if she hadn't fallen.

"I'm tired. I need to sleep. Can you pick up Poppy from Natasha's later? Don't tell her what's happened, not yet. Just tell her there's been an emergency at work. I don't want her worrying or seeing me like this."

"Natasha will keep hold of Poppy. I don't need to leave."

"There's no benefit in you just sitting there while I'm sleeping, is there? I'd rather Poppy was able to sleep in her own bed."

He bit down on his lower lip. "I don't want to leave you."

"I'll be fine. I just need to rest."

All she wanted was to retreat inside herself. She'd pull herself together eventually—she had a job and a family who needed her—but right now all she wanted to do was withdraw with her loss.

"Okay, as long as you're sure."

He seemed uncertain, but he leaned down and kissed her on the forehead. "Let me know if you need anything. I'm just on the end of the phone."

"Thanks."

Chapter Thirty-Three

F rances let out a yawn and set down the book she was reading.

"I'm heading up to bed," she told Matthew. "I'm shattered."

"Okay, love. I'm coming up right after you. I'll just watch the end of this." He nodded at some show he was watching about fishing.

Frances was happy to leave him to it. She poured herself a fresh glass of water to take up to bed with her and then went upstairs to the bathroom. She relieved herself, brushed her teeth, and washed her face, then went into the bedroom in search of a hairband so she could tie her hair up.

She froze.

One of her books sat on her bedside table.

Her stomach lurched. It was a copy of *A Perfect Death*. She hadn't put that book there. Why would she? It was one she'd written years ago, and while she had her author copies, they were all lining her bookshelves in her office. She'd given one to the detective, but otherwise she had no reason to take another one down, never mind leave it next to her bed.

Crazily, she picked it up and flicked to the front to see if it was signed. She remembered signing the copy for the detective. She had no idea why she thought it might be the same copy, but she needed to reassure herself that it wasn't.

Behind her, she heard Matt come up the stairs and use the bathroom. A moment later, he appeared in the bedroom, still brushing his teeth. He had an annoying habit of being unable to stay in one place while he was doing so and preferred to pace around the house instead.

"Did you put that there?" she asked, her voice trembling.

"What?" He paused brushing his teeth long enough to answer.

"That copy of *A Perfect Death*."

"No, why would I?"

"Well, someone did, and it certainly wasn't me."

"You probably took it down to fact-check some details and forgot you left it there."

Her heart was beating faster, and her palms had grown clammy. "I didn't! I'd have remembered something like that, Matt. Someone has left that book there for me."

He raised an eyebrow. "You're saying someone came into the house? Without us noticing?"

"They must have! What other explanation is there?"

If only the damned cameras had been installed already. She would have caught the son of a bitch on camera, and then she could have shown it to Matt. She'd have actual proof that this wasn't all in her head.

"That you forgot you moved it? Isn't the simplest explanation normally the right one?"

Not this time it wasn't.

Panic overwhelmed her. She couldn't think. Her chest grew tight, and her lungs seized up. She pressed her hand to her chest.

"I'm having a heart attack. Oh God. I can't breathe."

He placed his hand against her back, trying to reassure her. "No, you're not, Frances. It's a panic attack. You've had them before."

"No, this is different. It feels different. Oh, the pain."

It was as though someone had wrapped barbed wire around her heart and lungs and was pulling it ever tighter. Terror clutched her. This was how her father had died. He'd been alive one minute and gone the next. That was going to be her, too. She was going to black out and she'd never wake up again.

"You need to call an ambulance. Now!"

Was he just going to watch her die? Just stand there, doing nothing? Was this what he wanted? To be finally free of her?

Something about her utter terror must have finally got through to him as he stood and hurried over to where he'd left his phone on his side of the bed.

Frances was only vaguely aware of the conversation he was having with the operator. Her ears were filled with the rushing of her blood, and everything felt distant and strange. She dropped to her hands and knees on the floor, the soft carpet beneath her palms. Her vision drew in at the edges, and her mind kept spinning, and she gave in to darkness.

• • • •

SHE BECAME AWARE OF voices and people standing around her.

"What's her name?" a strange male voice asked.

This jolted her awake with renewed panic. Why was there a man in her room?

Her husband's voice followed. "Frances."

The stranger again. "Frances, my name is Dave, and I'm a paramedic. Do you mind if we take a look at you?"

Inwardly, she relaxed a fraction. Of course, she'd been yelling for Matt to call an ambulance, and he had. The pain from her chest had gone. She still felt weak and a little shaky, but otherwise she was all right. How long had she been out for?

"I think she wants to sit up," Matt said.

Two sets of hands helped her to sitting. Her hair hung over her face, and she pushed it away.

"I'm okay," she said quietly.

Now it was over, she felt stupid and embarrassed. She wished Matt hadn't listened to her when she'd yelled for an ambulance, but she guessed she hadn't given him much choice.

They picked her up off the floor so she could sit on the edge of the bed. She sensed Matt studying her, and she wanted to curl up into a ball and vanish. She was also aware of the book still sitting on her bedside table—the book she'd insisted she hadn't put there.

What if it had been Matt who'd left the book? What if a part of him was enjoying this? Weren't there people who got off on someone they cared about being ill? There was a name for it—Munchausen's, or something. Could he be the one who was messing with her? Perhaps he liked the attention, or that she depended on him so much, or that it made him the strong one. He had the opportunity to mess with her, didn't he? What if he'd been the one standing in the back garden that night? What if he'd told her that he'd been staying at his brother's place only so he could play tricks on her?

No, this was a crazy way of thinking, even she knew that. How would he have known she'd be awake at that time? It wasn't as though he'd just hang out in the garden all night in case she got up.

She found herself staring at him.

"You okay?" he asked, the three lines between his eyebrows deepening.

She was sure those lines hadn't been there only twelve months before. Was she the cause of them? Maybe Pete had been right when he'd said she was aging his brother.

Christ, what was she thinking? Matt wouldn't do this to her. He loved her.

Didn't he?

The paramedic, Dave, ran her through some questions and checked her pulse and blood pressure. "We can take you in," he offered, "have a doctor look you over?"

She shook her head. "No, I don't want to waste any more of your time. I'm sure you've got more important people to look after."

"You're important," he said. "Your husband said you're an author, is that right? Anything I might have read?"

Matt must have explained what had brought on the panic attack—one of her own books.

"Probably not," she admitted. "Most of my readers are women above the age of fifty."

He chuckled at that. "Well, I'll still keep an eye out for your name. My wife always likes a good book to read when we go on holiday."

The paramedics packed away their gear. Matt thanked them again and saw them out. A moment later, he returned to the bedroom where Frances remained in the same position.

"See," he said, "I told you it was just a panic attack."

"I don't need to hear 'I told you so' right now, Matt. It was still fucking frightening, and it still doesn't explain how that book got on my bedside table."

He sighed and picked it up. "I'll put it back on the bookshelf."

"Don't. Throw it in the bin. The outside bin."

He raised his eyebrows. "Are you serious?"

"Deadly. I never want to see it again." She thought of something else. "When are those cameras arriving?"

"Soon. Tomorrow, I think."

She chewed on a piece of dried skin beside her thumbnail. "If we'd had them installed already, we'd have caught whoever put the book there."

"Or we wouldn't have caught anyone, and it would have proven this is all in your head."

"Or it wouldn't have caught anyone because you were the one who put it there." She'd blurted the words before she'd even had the chance to think them through.

He froze, and the tension in the room seemed to crackle. "Are you serious right now?"

"I am. Were you the one who put the book there? Answer the question, Matt."

He threw up the hand not holding the book. "No, of course I didn't. Jesus Christ, it's just a fucking book."

"What about your brother?"

His confusion deepened. "Pete? Why would Pete have anything to do with this?"

"He came to see me the other day under some pretence that you'd forgotten your bank card."

"Oh. He wasn't pretending. I *had* forgotten my card."

"Seemed to me like he'd used it as a good excuse to come over and tell me what a crappy wife I am, how you'd be happier without me, and apparently I'm just sponging off you."

Matt rolled his eyes. "Oh, for God's sake, Frances, he did not say all of that."

Her mouth fell open. "Are you calling me a liar now?"

"Not a liar, no. You're just not very good at interpreting the things Pete says. I admit he can be a little brusque at times, but he's a good man."

She snorted with laughter at that. "Yeah, right."

He let out a sigh. "I'm not having this fight. I want to go to bed and get some sleep. Some of us have got real jobs to get up for in the morning."

She jerked back like he'd slapped her. "So you're saying I don't have a real job now?"

"You don't have a nine-to-five, no. You can stay in bed all day if you wanted."

"I don't, though, do I? I work hard."

He shrugged. "I don't know what you do. You might sleep all day."

Anger burst up through her. "Do you really think I could write as many books as I do if I was sleeping all day? For fuck's sake, Matt, it sounds like you agree with Pete, in that you think I do nothing and just sponge off you."

He shook his head. "I'm not talking about this now. Come to bed."

But she was raging. "No fucking way." She jumped to her feet. "I don't want to be in the same room as you, never mind the same bed. I don't even want to be in the same house. Actually, I think I'm going to get out of here."

"Don't be ridiculous, Frances. Where are you going?"

She didn't even know. All she knew was that she didn't want to be anywhere near him. She shoved past him and stormed down the stairs, pushed her feet into some shoes, and snatched up her car keys. She didn't know where she was going or what she planned to do when she got there, she just wanted to be away from her husband.

The husband who might be trying to drive her insane.

Chapter Thirty-Four

The doctors discharged Erica the following morning.

She went home briefly to take a shower and wash her hair and try to make herself feel half-human before returning to the office. She didn't know what excuse Shawn would have given to the rest of the team for her sudden absence, but she assumed he'd told DCI Gibbs the truth.

Shawn was already in the office. Poppy already at school. The house was mercifully empty. She didn't want to face either of them.

She knew she was shutting them out, but it was all she could do to hold herself together.

She wished there was a way of getting through this without everyone knowing, but of course they'd find out eventually. She didn't want sympathy; she just wanted to get on with things.

She dressed in her trousers, sticking with the maternity ones, as her stomach still felt tender and she was still having cramps. She'd taken some painkillers to help. She didn't want to think about what they'd lost. It was easier to focus on work than her homelife. Telling Poppy would break her heart. Poor Poppy had thought she was finally going to be a big sister, and now her dreams would be dashed, too.

Maybe Erica should have stayed home, but she couldn't bear it. She hadn't gone as far as buying anything for the baby, knowing it had been too early, but in a way, it was as though a small piece of her home was suddenly missing.

Though she knew no one would know exactly what had happened, she still felt horribly self-conscious going into the office. Her team had probably noticed her sudden departure yesterday afternoon and would wonder what had happened and if everything was okay.

She put on a brave smile and kept her chin high. Brisk and businesslike, she wouldn't entertain anyone asking after her. Too much kindness would reduce her to tears.

She did that morning's roll call.

"Right, can anyone bring me up to speed on any developments from yesterday?" She assumed someone would have mentioned if there had been anything groundbreaking.

They went through the details on local CCTV, bank and phone records, and any potential witnesses they'd spoken to. Her brain kept trying to bring her back to what had happened, especially when a fresh cramp went through her. The painkillers had taken the edge off, but that was all. It was understandable that she'd still be feeling tender.

When the meeting was over, Shawn pulled her to one side.

"What are you doing?" he said.

"What do you mean? I'm doing my job."

Shawn stared at her. "How can you act like this?"

"Like what?"

He gestured up and down her body. "Like this. Putting on a suit and coming in to work like nothing has happened."

"What am I supposed to do? Lie in bed crying all day? I don't have time for that. I've got a job to do, and it's a goddamned important one. Someone is killing innocent people, and I need to stop them."

"*We* need to stop them. It's not just you working on this case."

"No, but I'm the SIO. It's important that I'm present."

A muscle in his jaw flexed. "You never wanted this baby."

She closed her eyes briefly and then opened them again, fixing on his. "I'll admit that I've struggled with it, but that's allowed. It was unexpected, and yes, it came as a shock. But that doesn't mean I didn't want it, and I'd have loved it just as much when he or she arrived."

"You put yourself in danger. I told you not to, but you wouldn't listen. You didn't want anything to change." Tears filmed his dark eyes.

"What are you saying? That I did this on purpose? That I put myself in harm's way so I'd lose the baby?"

He turned his face from her. "That's not what I'm saying..."

"Isn't it?" Self-righteous anger boiled inside her. He was hurting, but so was she.

"It's just that you've barely seemed affected. You spent one night in hospital, and then you were straight back to work."

"So because I haven't spent all day weeping in bed, that means I don't care? I have to be strong, Shawn. I've always had to be strong. I keep things together. That's what I do."

He shook his head. "Not with me. You don't have to be strong with me."

"Don't I? You just implied that I'd deliberately allowed a man to attack me so I'd lose this pregnancy. Don't you realise how much that hurts me? As if I haven't been through enough. This is why I can't let my guard down—ever. Because the moment I do, someone out there is going to do their best to tear me down."

He rubbed his thumb against a vein in his temple and looked away from her. "You're not the only one in pain, Erica. I wanted this baby. I wanted it more than anything."

"You always said you were fine with our family as it was—with me and Poppy. Now everything has changed."

"Yeah," he said sadly, "I guess it has."

She released a breath. "I can't do this right now. I have a job to do."

"A job that takes priority over everything else. Over me. Over the baby we might have had. Over your own daughter."

She jerked back as though he'd slapped her.

"How fucking dare you."

He pressed his lips together and shook his head. "I think we both need some space."

"How is that supposed to happen? We work together." She didn't add, and live together, for fear of what he might say.

His tone was cool. "We can both be professional, can't we?"

"I guess we have no choice." This was what she'd always been afraid of. She was going to lose him, both at home and work, and she had no idea how to fix this. Was he right? Had she, even if it was only subconsciously, put herself in danger because deep down she hadn't wanted to have the baby?

Was she really that cold inside?

Chapter Thirty-Five

A couple of hours later, DC Jon Howard approached Erica's desk.

"I've just had a call from DS Wakley in Missing Persons. The crime author who came to see you about the murders is missing. Her husband reported her missing this morning. He says he's been trying her phone, but it's just gone straight through to voicemail."

"Is that unusual for her, to not make contact, I mean?"

"Yes, according to her husband. He says they had a fight last night and she stormed out, but she hasn't been heard from since. He says she took her car. But when she still wasn't back this morning, and wasn't answering her phone, he called us."

Erica twisted her lips. "Maybe she just doesn't want to talk to him? That would be understandable if they had a fight. I assume he's checked with family and friends."

"He says Frances doesn't really have any. That she's quite an introverted person. Both her parents died when she was younger, so she doesn't have any family apart from him. He claims she wouldn't go anywhere without telling him, at least not for this length of time."

"She could easily just be holed up in a hotel somewhere."

"True, but since she has a connection to this case, I thought we might want to dig a little deeper."

Erica pursed her lips, considering this. "She did say that she had the feeling someone was following her, but she also admitted that she had issues with her mental health."

"You've got to admit that the ways these murders have mirrored her books have been strange. More than strange." He shrugged. "MisPer are working on the case, but I asked them to keep us updated."

"Thanks," she said. "Hopefully, she'll show up soon and it's nothing to worry about."

It did niggle at Erica, though. The author had been extremely anxious when she'd come to talk to her. Even if there was nothing in it, Frances had *believed* there was. She hoped Frances hadn't done anything stupid. It didn't sound as though she had much of a support system in place, if she only had her husband.

She wished she'd paid the author more attention when she'd come to speak to her, but she'd had other things going on in her head.

That part hadn't changed. Her fight with Shawn left her sick to her stomach, and she fought the urge to break down in tears. Maybe she should be home, grieving over the loss of her pregnancy, and maybe even the loss of her relationship, but she couldn't allow herself to break down. People needed her.

She did her best to concentrate on case files but wasn't left alone for long.

Her phone rang, and she answered it. "DI Swift."

"It's DS Wakley in Missing Persons. I wanted to keep you updated about the MisPer case we're investigating. A Frances Gilchrist. I believe she's a person of interest to you."

"Yes, that's right. She's possibly connected to the two murder cases we're investigating. Do you have news about her?"

"We've found her car in a car park near Beachy Head in Dover. We got a couple of hits on the ANPR in the early hours of the morning. Looks like she drove down there. We've got local police checking it out, but no sign of her so far. No sign of a body either."

Erica's stomach dropped. Beachy Head, on the Dover cliffs, was a notorious spot for suicides. Had Frances really taken that route out? It made sense. If her husband was the only person in her life, and they'd fought, and she'd believed that one strut of support had been removed, maybe she'd felt she had no choice. That, combined with the obvious mental distress she'd been in about the murders, and her history of mental health, meant it made sense.

"Shit, that's awful. I really hope she's found alive and well. Has anyone spoken to her husband yet?"

"I've got a couple of my officers going around to the house to speak to him."

She let out a sigh. "I wish I had done more when she came to see me. I could see she was troubled, but it all just seemed so fantastical. The idea that someone was using her books to inspire their crimes. I thought it must just be a coincidence."

"Did you read them?"

"Not the whole things, but I read the scenes she was talking about. I mean, there were definitely similarities—extreme similarities—but I'm sure if we went through every murder that's ever happened, we could probably find a similar one written in a book somewhere."

"You're right," he said down the line.

"Will you let me know what he says?"

"Of course."

She ended the call feeling terrible. Should she have done more? Maybe she hadn't taken Frances's fears seriously enough. They'd clearly been real to her. But did Frances need a therapist more than she needed a detective?

What other reason would Frances have for going to Beachy Head than ending her life? Would her body have been found by now or not? She wasn't completely sure how far in the tide came, if the body would be washed out to sea, or if it should have been found on the line of sand and rocks at the bottom of the cliff?

Poor Frances. She really had believed those murders had been connected to her books. Had she killed herself out of guilt? She'd felt as though if she'd never written those scenes those two men would still be alive.

Chapter Thirty-Six

Frances's head was pounding. Her mouth dry. Nausea washed through her. The room seemed to spin.

It was dark.

Where was she?

She tried to piece together the last of her memories. She'd had a fight with Matt and stormed out. Goddamn it. What had happened then?

Gradually, the memory came back to her.

She remembered getting in her car, not even thinking about where she was going. All she'd wanted was some space and distance to think. She'd considered going to a hotel for the night and not telling him where she was so that he'd worry.

She'd *wanted* him to worry.

Now look at her.

She'd been driving, and there had been something in the road. At first she'd thought it was a black rubbish bag, and then, as she'd got closer, a dog. It had been dark and difficult to see in the headlights. But then, as she was almost upon it, she realised it had been a person.

Not thinking, she'd slammed on the brakes and jumped out of the car. She'd run to check if the person was all right, and, as she'd crouched to see, he'd grabbed her, hooked his arm around her neck. Choked her.

She didn't remember much at all after that.

The reality of her situation sank in. No, no, no. Someone had snatched her. Taken her.

Frances reached down to where her leg was attached to something. In the dark, she patted around. There was metal around her ankle. A handcuff. A chain.

What the fuck?

She reached out and felt around her. The walls were soft and spongy. With her thoughts as thick as soup, she didn't quite put together what it was at first, but then the realisation dawned. It was soundproofing.

This was not good. This was really not good.

Somewhere she experienced the perverse thought: *I was right!*

She hadn't just been being paranoid when she'd thought someone was following her or when she'd spotted someone in the garden. It had been real. Someone had been messing with her.

She followed the handcuff around her ankle and patted along the chain. The other end of the cuff was around a metal pipe. She yanked on it as hard as she could, letting out a yell of frustration, but it didn't budge.

"Hey!" she screamed. "Let me out!"

She knew it was futile, but that didn't stop her from screaming for help. She'd been too shocked and frightened to cry, but as her throat grew raw and her chest ached from shouting, the tears took hold.

What did they want from her?

Was it the same person who'd killed those two men? Had she been right in her belief that the killer had copied the scenes from her books? But he hadn't killed her—he'd brought her here instead.

Why?

Frances had the horrible feeling she'd find out soon enough.

Chapter Thirty-Seven

Frances must have fallen asleep.

She came round, slowly at first, and then all at once. She'd been lying asleep on the floor, her head on her hands, her chained leg stuck out behind her at an awkward angle. Both hands were dead, and pins and needles ran up her arms. She groaned and did her best to sit up, flapping her hands and trying to curl and uncurl her fingers to get some feeling back in them.

The metal of the cuff had dug into her ankle, the pressure made worse as she'd slept and not realised how much weight she'd put on it. Now it had pressed deep into her skin, leaving a painful groove.

How long had she been asleep for? She had no idea. With no light in here, and no way of telling the time, she didn't know if it was still night or if morning had arrived.

She still didn't know who had taken her or why. Surely they'd make themselves known soon. But what would happen when they did? Would they kill her? Had the other victims been brought to this place before they'd been murdered?

She wanted to know what was going on, but she was also terrified of her kidnapper making himself known. Himself. Yes, definitely a man. She didn't doubt that for a second. She could sense his masculinity from the first moment he'd grabbed her.

She did her best to explore her surroundings, to use her hands to feel around the room. But the way her ankle was chained to the pipes meant she could only reach a certain distance. As far as she could tell, there was nothing else in the room with her—just the strange, padded walls, and the thick, spongy carpet beneath her.

Movement came at the door.

A lock unclicked.

Her heart crawled up her throat, and her stomach dropped. She pressed herself back against the cold radiator behind her, as though she thought she might vanish into it.

The light behind framed his figure in a silhouette.

A shot of recognition went through her. There was something familiar about his shape and the way he was standing.

Her eyes gradually got used to the change in light.

It was her editor.

"Blaire?" Her heart soared. She didn't know how he'd found her, but he had. Maybe he'd seen the person grab her and had followed whoever had taken her. "Oh my God, Blaire. Please help me. Someone's chained me up in here." She yanked her ankle. "Please, find something to get this undone."

He didn't move.

"Quickly," she cried. "I don't know how long it'll be before the bastard comes to get me. I think he killed those two men. Please, Blaire. Do something!"

She choked on those final words. Tears that had filled her eyes now spilled down her cheeks.

The reason he was doing nothing gradually dawned on her.

He was the person who'd taken her and chained her up in this room.

"Blaire, no, please, no. Why are you doing this to me?"

He stepped into the room, and she noted that he had a bag slung across his shoulder.

"I have a gift for you."

She didn't reply, not sure what would be the right thing to say.

Why was this happening? She'd always respected him. She'd never had any suspicion that he'd be capable of doing something like this. Did this mean that Blaire was also the one responsible for killing those two men? No, surely not. Even now, chained up like this, with him standing in front of her, she couldn't make those two possibilities fuse.

He reached into his bag and pulled out a laptop.

It had been the last thing she'd been expecting to see. A knife, or a gun, perhaps, but not a laptop. If it had access to the internet, she could use it to call for help.

He must have read her expression. "Don't get excited. There's no Wi-Fi for you to log into. It's not only because I don't want you to use it to contact someone. I also don't want you to get distracted."

Distracted? What the hell was he talking about?

"I-I don't understand."

The normally composed, friendly man had been replaced by a monster.

"You're here to write it." He shoved the laptop—an expensive MacBook Air—at her.

She was confused. "Write what?"

"Our story. My story. The one I've created."

Her mind blurred, her thoughts fighting against one another to try and figure out what he meant. Panic made it difficult to think. She was terrified that he'd hurt her if she said the wrong thing.

"I don't know what you're talking about," she blurted.

"Yes, you do." He dropped to a crouch to bring himself level with her. "You told me about it yourself when you came to my office. I was impressed you recognised it so quickly, but then you always did have a good eye for detail."

Her breath quickened, and she edged back again. "Do you mean the murders?"

"Of course. What else? I want you to write this story." He put the laptop on the floor and slid it towards her.

She stared at it as though it might morph into a wild animal and attack her.

He was crazy. Completely insane. How had she not noticed this about him before? She'd always thought he was enthusiastic and passionate, but not to this level. This was completely nuts.

"It's a way to immortality, don't you think?" he continued. "To have your words printed in a book. People die, but as long as a book is being printed, a piece of them will always carry on."

"Bu-but—if I write your name in a book and link it to those murders, everyone will know what you've done."

"I thought you were brighter than this, Frances. Of course you won't use real names. You can use my middle name instead. It'll be enough for me, just knowing that it's out there."

What the hell was he planning? To keep her here long enough to write a whole book, and then he'd publish it? How long would that take? Months? And what would he do with her after it was finished?

Her eyes filled with fresh tears. "This is insane. I'm not writing for you."

His jaw locked, and he rose to standing.

"Don't make me hurt you, Frances."

"No, no, please don't," she said hurriedly. "I'll write whatever you want. Just tell me what to type."

"No!" he roared. She'd only made him angrier. "*You're* the one who needs to write it. I can't write my own book. Don't you think I'd have done it by now if I was able to? What is it they say? Those who can, do? I might be able to edit other people's stories, but I've never been able to write my own. Now, open the laptop."

With shaking hands, she drew the machine towards her and opened it up. The screen blinked to life. There was no password needed. It opened up on a new Word document. That empty page stared ominously back at her.

Her hands shook.

How was she supposed to do this? Her mind was a complete blank. He'd read all her work, of course he had, so it wasn't as though she could just churn out something she'd written before.

"I want to *feel* something, Frances. I want this to be the best thing you've ever written."

Tears streamed down her cheeks. "I-I can't. I don't know what to write. I need some time to think."

He stormed over to her and grabbed her by the hair, yanking hard enough to make pain spear through her scalp. "We don't have time!"

She let out a shriek and clawed at his hands, trying to get him off again. "Please, stop, stop. I'll do it."

He'd be interviewed, wouldn't he, when they realised she was missing? The police would question everyone who was connected to her. What would he say? Would he speak about how distraught he was to find out she'd disappeared? What would happen to her book sales? Would people get curious about the young—ish—crime author who'd vanished? Would they buy more of her books, hoping to see into her mind? Would people speculate about what had happened?

She'd become a victim in one of her own books, literally.

She felt like she was losing her mind.

He released her hair, and she put her hand to the top of her head and winced. A chunk was missing, and her scalp was wet. When she pulled her fingers away, they were tipped red with blood.

How far would he go? Would he kill her? What would happen if she ever did finish this book? It wasn't as though he was going to let her go.

Blaire stepped back and folded his arms across his chest. "What are you waiting for?"

How was she going to do this? It took her months to write a full-length book. Was he really going to keep her here for this long, with her ankle chained to the pipes? She was his prisoner.

She thought of something else.

"How are you going to explain where you got this book from? It'll incriminate you."

"I'll say I found it on a flash drive, that you'd sent it to me before you went missing, but I must have tossed it in with a load of other submissions."

"That won't work. Digital forensics will be able to tell when the file was written and updated."

Her research meant she had at least a half-decent knowledge of these things.

Was she talking herself out of his reason to keep her alive? If she convinced him that the book wasn't worth writing, or that it would get him locked up, it wasn't like he'd just let her go.

He'd kill her.

"I'll wait until the police aren't interested anymore. People go missing all the time. They'll move on to someone else once the initial excitement dies down. You don't have anyone who'll care enough to keep pushing it, do you, Frances? Your husband will forget about you soon enough. I've met him, remember. He's only interested in himself."

"That's not true."

But in the back of her mind, she wondered if it *was* true. How long would Matt search for her? Would he be heartbroken at her loss?

"Besides, after I brought you here, I drove your car down to Dover. People will think you've jumped."

She sucked in a breath. "What?"

"They won't find a body, of course, but that's how it'll seem."

Her eyes filled with fresh tears. He was right. People would think that. They all thought she was crazy anyway—what with her fears over her health, and then her believing that the recent murders in the area were linked to her books.

She almost laughed. To think she'd been terrified of a heart attack or cancer getting her, when instead it was a character from one of her books, or at least would be once she'd written it.

He continued, "So they'll close the case, and sometime after I'll find the new manuscript. People will love it. A new book from Frances Gilchrist—a book from beyond the grave. Imagine the sort of publicity that'll come with it. Everyone will lap it up, and they won't even know it's my story. Or perhaps I should say *our* story. We'll both live forever within these pages."

"And if I don't write it? If I can't write it?"

He eyed her coldly. "Then I won't have any more use for you, Frances."

Chapter Thirty-Eight

A call from the desk sergeant came through to Erica's phone.

"Someone is here to speak to you," the sergeant said. "He says his name is Matthew Gilchrist."

Matthew Gilchrist? The author's husband. What did he want?

"Thanks, I'll be right out," she said and ended the call.

She left her desk to go and meet the man who'd come to see her.

Matthew Gilchrist was an attractive man in his forties. He had the air of being someone who expected people to look up to him. But though he was doing an excellent job of holding himself together, Erica didn't miss the signs of strain around his mouth and brow, and the bloodshot eyes that indicated he'd been crying, or the shadows beneath them that spoke of his sleepless night.

This was a man who was worried about his wife.

"DI Swift?" he asked.

She nodded. "Come on through. I understand you want to speak to me."

"That's right."

She led him into a private room so they could talk and gestured for him to sit.

"I found your card on my wife's bedside table," he said. "She must have spoken to you before she went missing."

"Yes, she did, but I'm not the person dealing with her case."

"I don't care. She spoke to you for a reason. She kept your card for a reason. It was right next to where she slept at night. Don't tell me that someone keeps something like that if they think they're never going to use it again?"

A flush of shame washed over her. "I didn't take her seriously enough."

"Neither did I, and I'm her husband. You can't blame yourself."

"I really do hope Frances shows up somewhere safe, but that location where her car was found..." Erica shook her head.

"Frances hasn't killed herself, if that's what you're thinking. I'm not saying that I believe she's safe, because she'd have either come home or got in touch if she was, but she didn't kill herself."

Erica paused, considering her next words. "Your wife has issues with mental health. Is that right?"

"Yes, but I still don't believe that means she'd kill herself. You don't know Frances. She's terrified of death. Absolutely terrified of it. It's the thing that controls her life, and there's no way she'd willingly choose to die."

"You say she's scared of death, but isn't that what she writes about? People being killed, that is."

He nodded and glanced down at his hands. "I think it's her way of having control over it. Yes, people are killed in her books, but then the culprits responsible for the deaths are always caught and dealt with. It's like that kind of therapy where if you're scared of spiders, the therapist makes you go into a room full of spiders."

"Immersion therapy," Erica filled in.

"That's right. Writing is Frances's way of creating her own immersion therapy. But she wouldn't kill herself. There's no possible way. Something has happened to her." A tear slipped from his right eye, and he batted it away. "She thought someone was following her, stalking her, sending her notes. And then there was all that stuff about those two murders being like ones in her books. I know she was paranoid, and it's probably only a coincidence, but it's not a coincidence that she's now gone missing."

"We found her car down by Dover Cliffs."

"It doesn't matter. Anyone could have moved her car there. All they needed to do was get in it and drive."

"I expect the detective in MisPer who is working on her case will be trying to get an ANPR hit on the plate where the person driving is visible. There might be a chance we can get a picture of whoever was driving. If it is her..." Erica let her words trail off. She didn't need to finish what she was saying for him to know what she meant.

They didn't seem to affect him, though. He remained resolute. "It won't be her. It won't."

Erica hoped for both his and Frances's sake that he was right.

Chapter Thirty-Nine

B laire had left her alone for hours.

Frances didn't know where he'd gone—perhaps he'd even gone into work and acted like everything was fine and he was completely normal—but she was sure he hadn't been here.

Wherever *here* was.

The laptop was brand new, and the charge on it gave her a full twelve hours, but she hadn't been given a lead, so she turned the brightness right down on the screen to preserve the battery.

Her fears over the laptop dying had less to do with her wanting it to write and more to do with her not wanting to be shut back in the dark. The glare from the screen was the only thing lighting the room, and if it died, then she'd be back in the pitch-black.

Despite him telling her there was no Wi-Fi, she'd still done everything she could to find one she could access. How could there be nothing? Had he put in some kind of blocker as well? She wished she was more technologically minded so she could hack it or something, but the truth was navigating her way around a Word document was the height of her skills.

Where the hell was she? She didn't recognise anything, and because of the soundproofing, she couldn't hear anything either. She'd tried yelling and screaming until her throat was sore and her voice had grown hoarse, but Blaire hadn't come back in to try to shut her up. That made her think he believed the soundproofing would work and he wasn't worried that anyone would hear her. She was wasting her time by trying.

She'd stared at the empty page for what felt like forever, her mind a complete blank. Where did she even start? Though she'd already written a story where a body had been found on a spike, this would be the true story of a copycat killer, except the murders he'd copied had been fictional.

Her fingers trembled as she rested them against the keyboard. She guessed the best place to start was where she began most of her novels—at the discovery of the murder victim—except this time the victim wasn't someone from her imagination. He'd been a very real person.

Tears slid down her cheeks, and she sniffed and wiped them away.

That poor man. He'd lost his life because of her, and because of Blaire. He'd only been young, too, in his early twenties with his whole life ahead of him.

She remembered what Blaire had said about immortality. Was she giving the victim at least a small nod at it by writing his story?

Because she'd been following the murder so closely, she knew many of the details. The rest she could conjure up because she knew that Blaire had used a scene from one of her older books as inspiration. Of course, she couldn't write exactly what the poor victim had been thinking or know what his final moments had been. It occurred to her that Blaire might be able to fill in those details—after all, hadn't he been the one to follow the young man to where he'd been killed?—but she didn't want to involve him any more than she had to.

How had Blaire known him? Why had Blaire chosen that particular young man?

She took a shaky breath and closed her eyes and did her best to conjure the words. Slowly, she began to type.

Her hands shook, and she struggled to hit the right keys. Every other word was underlined in red where she'd typed a mistake.

It felt stilted and false, the idea that she was recreating an actual person's murder not sitting right with her. But she knew she needed to press on. The page was littered with typos, but she didn't dare go back and fix them in case she ruined what little flow she had.

Instead of writing the discovery of the body, she found herself writing from the victim's point of view. Of him leaving the pub and getting some food. She didn't know the reason why he'd ended up where he had, but she could picture the sense of someone following him, and she knew exactly who the person had been.

When she got to the part where he was murdered, she broke down in floods of tears, letting out a howl of grief, her whole body shaking with it. She hadn't known the man, but that didn't mean she didn't feel for him. Wasn't that part of what it was to write—to be able to channel another's thoughts and feeling through her fingers, even if normally they weren't real?

Frances couldn't manage anymore. Sobbing, she pushed the laptop to one side and curled up in a ball.

It suddenly occurred to her that she hadn't given any thought to her health ever since she'd been grabbed. All those years of overanalysing every headache, every muscle twinge, every heart palpitation, and now she in a genuinely life-threatening situation, and she hadn't thought about any of those things. She barked out cold laughter. Maybe this was all that was needed to be cured? To be held in a room by a madman and forced to write.

Hours passed. Frances was hungry and thirsty, and she needed to pee, but she had nowhere to do so. Would he take her to the bathroom when he got back? Could she hold on long enough for that to happen? She was at a point of it being painful now.

It felt like a lifetime had gone by, but finally the door opened again.

Frances pushed herself back up to sitting and huddled against the cold radiator.

Blaire had brought her a pre-packaged sandwich and a bottle of water. She still had a headache, but that was hardly surprising.

"I need to use the bathroom."

He nodded. "I thought of that." He left the room again and returned with a bucket. Was he serious?

"I can't use that."

"Then you'll have to go on the floor, and I'd suggest you refrain from doing that or this will become very unpleasant for the both of us." He set the bucket down beside her. "I'll give you some privacy."

He'd left her the sandwich and water as well.

"Shit. You bastard. You absolute fucking bastard."

She had no choice. She was painfully desperate now, and with the promise of release so close, her bladder was giving her no choice. She yanked down her trousers and underwear and squatted over the bucket. She sobbed in relief.

Was this really her life now?

With business taken care of, she moved the bucket as far away as she could, then cracked open the bottle of water and gulped it down in one.

A knock came at the door. "You done in there?"

That he was being polite enough to check on her modesty, but yet expected her to piss in a bucket, almost made her laugh all over again.

"Yeah," she called back through gritted teeth. "I'm done."

Perhaps she should have kept hold of the bucket and thrown both it and its contents at him the moment he walked back through the door. But she knew it wouldn't kill him, and she was still chained to the pipes. What if she hurt him badly and no one knew where she was? She could end up dying in here.

No, it was better that she play his games, try to keep him happy for as long as possible.

She thought of what he'd said about him parking her car down near Dover cliffs. Would people really think she'd killed herself? Matt wouldn't. He knew how terrified she was of death. She'd never choose to go willingly. Would the police believe him, though? Or would they just see her history of mental health struggles and stop looking?

The door opened, and he re-entered. He screwed up his nose at the bucket and then gingerly picked it up and set it in the hallway outside.

"Right," he said, clapping once. "Let's see what you've come up with."

For one crazy moment, she was transported back to his office. She felt like she'd just taken a seat at his desk and was about to talk him through her latest manuscript. Her grip on reality felt too loose, like it was pulling away at the edges and would collapse all around her.

"I-I don't know if it's any good."

She picked up the slimline laptop and slid it across the floor towards him.

He opened the screen and began to read.

She'd never felt so nervous in her life. After all the years she'd spent submitting manuscripts and waiting to hear from editors, she'd never thought she might actually throw up while she waited for feedback. Her stomach churned, and her heart banged against the inside of her ribcage.

She'd never been great at writing under pressure. Any time she'd had a deadline looming, she'd found herself staring at the computer screen with barely a thought in her head.

His gaze remained locked on the screen, his eyes darting back and forth as he took in her words. She couldn't read his expression at all. It was completely blank. Did he hate it? Did he love it?

It certainly wasn't her best work, but then how was she supposed to write a masterpiece under these conditions? Chained to a pipe and pissing in a bucket.

Blaire got to the end of the chapter she'd written, shut the lid again, and closed his eyes.

Frances held her breath.

He shook his head. "I should break your fingers for such a poor attempt, but you need those to write. I should gouge out your eyes as punishment, but again you need those."

She gulped a breath.

"No, please, I'm sorry. I'll do better. I promise."

"You insult me with this, Frances. Is that what you want? To insult and embarrass me? You think this pithy attempt is going to be the sort of work that people are still reading long after we're gone? I wouldn't publish this if you were the last author alive."

Her eyes filled with tears. "I'm sorry. I don't know how you think—"

He slammed his hand down on the top of the laptop, and she jumped.

"Don't blame me for your own failings. How fucking dare you. I've made your career. Your books would be nothing without my input, but does anyone ever think about who edits your mess? Do they even glance at my name? No, never."

Was he really a frustrated writer? Was that what he wanted—to have his name on the cover?

"We could write it together," she tried. "Maybe that would work better."

It was the wrong thing to say. "We *are* writing it together! What the fuck do you think is happening here?"

She shrank back. "Yes, of course. I know that."

"I'm hitting delete on this whole sorry mess."

"I-I'll try again. I'm sorry."

"Maybe you should lose your tongue. You don't need that to write."

Madness danced in his eyes. Would he really do it? Would he cut out her tongue?

She couldn't help it, she broke down, sobbing against her knees. Begging for her life. She didn't want to be here. She was stuck in a nightmare she couldn't escape.

"I'm taking the laptop with me so I can charge it," he said. "I'm sure you appreciate that I'm a busy man and I've got people expecting me to be in meetings, so I'll return it to you when it's charged and I can get away."

Jesus Christ, he was going to work. Was he going to sit in the office and act like he was a normal human being? Would people mention that she was missing? How could he act like nothing was happening when he knew he had her chained in his home?

She tried to think of any connection that the police might make that would lead them to her but couldn't think of one. Had anyone seen him snatching her? She didn't think so, but wasn't it the police's job to find out things like that?

Unless, of course, what he'd told her about him making it seem like she'd killed herself was true. Then no one would be looking for her.

"I suggest you use that time to work out how you're going to improve on the sorry mess you started with. I don't want to be disappointed in you again."

She couldn't do this. She just couldn't. It didn't matter what he threatened her with—writing something well wasn't something she was capable of under these conditions. Maybe she could string a few sentences together, but that didn't mean they'd be any good.

Perhaps it would come to her in time. She imagined herself months from now, still shut in here, except she'd have pieces of her missing from where he'd cut off her toes, her ears, her lips, all as punishment.

Would she be driven mad by then? Or with no contact with anyone other than him, no television or internet, or even other books to read, perhaps then she'd find herself able to write. She might need the respite of vanishing into a story, even if it was *her* story. Maybe it would be the only thing that would keep her sane.

Except in this story, the good guy wasn't going to win.

Chapter Forty

E rica's phone rang.

"It's DS Wakley again," the voice on the other end of the line said. "I thought you'd want to know that we got a picture from the ANPR cameras for Frances Gilchrist's car. It's not a great image, and I've sent it over to digital forensics to try and get a better resolution, but at a first glance, I'd say there's a possibility that the person driving *isn't* Frances."

Erica sat up at that. "Do you have an image I can see?"

"I've just emailed it over to you."

She clamped the phone between her ear and shoulder as she ran her fingers over her keyboard to open the email. She clicked open the photograph and stared at it.

Sure enough, the image was fuzzy, but still possible to make out.

The person had the black hood of a zip-up pulled up over their head. If it was Frances driving, why would she bother to try and hide her identity? There was no sign of her blonde hair.

"Can we get the hands on the steering wheel blown up? Frances is married, and her husband said she never takes off her wedding or engagement rings. It's not clear in this picture, but I don't think the driver is wearing any rings."

"She could have removed them. Maybe left them somewhere for her husband?"

"It's possible, though he says she was still wearing them when she left. He really doesn't believe that there's any possibility of her killing herself."

"You believe him? That Frances Gilchrist wouldn't kill herself, I mean."

"I think I do. I spoke to her, remember. She really was convinced that those murders were connected to her books and that someone was stalking her. Maybe we didn't take her seriously enough. We put it down to a coincidence, but what if it wasn't?"

Had she failed Frances? She hadn't offered her any kind of protection, despite everything she'd said, and now she'd become like a victim in one of her own books.

Or was she about to embark on a wild goose chase and try to find a woman whose body was already in the sea somewhere at the bottom of the Dover cliffs?

"There's something else," Wakley said down the line. "We had her car impounded by forensics, and it's come back as being wiped of prints."

Erica frowned. "Would she have done that? What would have been the point? Have you ever thought to wipe your own car of prints? Of course not. The only reason it would be is if someone is trying to hide something."

"Like their own prints," he suggested.

"Exactly."

. . . .

THAT EVENING, ERICA and Shawn had had to break the news to Poppy, who'd been understandably devastated and had gone to bed in tears. Erica felt utterly drained, and all she wanted was to curl up next to her daughter and sleep as well, but she couldn't. There were things that needed to be discussed.

Once they knew she was asleep, they sat down to talk.

"I think I should move out," Shawn said.

"Seriously? You don't think that's a little much? What about Poppy? You're going to break her heart."

Poppy had been so small when her dad had died, she barely remembered him. Erica did her best to keep his memory alive, and his photographs still littered the walls, but the truth was that Shawn was the closest thing she'd had to a dad.

"I'll break *her* heart? What about *your* heart, Erica? Don't you give a shit?"

"Of course I do. How can you say that? But I'm always going to think of her first."

"And I'll always think of *you* first. You shut down on me. The moment that pregnancy test turned positive, it was like a wall went up. Do you know how hard it's been just being around you?"

She glanced away, knowing he was right. "What do you want me to say? That we'll try again?" Tears filled her eyes. "Because I'd be lying if I said I wanted that. The pregnancy was an accident, you know it was, and it was something that would be life-changing for me."

He threw up a hand. "It would have been life-changing for the both of us."

She shook her head. "Not in the same way. It just isn't the same. No matter how much you'd promise to help out, ultimately that baby would have been my responsibility. I've already gone through it once, and it was fucking hard. Neither of us want to give up our careers, but I'd have been the person who'd have given up the most."

He gritted his teeth. "This is what it's about? Your job?"

"No, it's about my *life*."

"It's my life, too."

She forced herself to soften her tone. "I'm sorry I hurt you, however much it was never intended. But I can't do or say what you want to fix this."

"Which is?"

"Tell you that we'll try again. I'm sorry."

Maybe it would be easier for her to bend, to give him what he wanted at her own sacrifice, but she couldn't bring herself to do it.

"I just need some time, Erica. Some space. Seeing you both at home and work...it's too much."

Her heart felt like it was breaking. "Where will you go?"

"I can stay with Jasmine and her mum, for the short-term anyway. I'm sure they'll be happy to have me."

She softened her tone. "Of course they will. I'm going to miss you. Poppy will, too. How will I explain this to her?"

"Just tell her the truth."

How ironic that he wanted her to tell a child the truth when he found it so hard to hear himself.

He acted as though she'd hurt him deliberately. Didn't he understand that she was hurting as well? She was the one who'd gone through a miscarriage. She was the one who'd been pregnant. Her body was crazy with hormones right now.

"Don't go yet, please," she begged him. "Just give it some time."

He drew a breath and closed his eyes. "Okay. I'll stay tonight, but I'm not making any promises."

She guessed that would have to be good enough.

Chapter Forty-One

E rica hadn't gone straight into the office the next day.
Things had been tense at home. Shawn was avoiding her and had slept on the sofa, then had left for work without her. Poppy had been quiet and upset. Everything felt like such a fucking mess, and at the same time her body was going through the hormone crash of a miscarriage.

Erica wanted to visit the spot where Frances Gilchrist's car had been found. It was a couple of hours' drive, but she didn't mind. Maybe, in part at least, she was using it as a good excuse to get out of the city. She wanted some space so she could breathe more deeply, to clear her head. As much as she loved London, sometimes it did her good to get away. Had Frances felt the same way? Had the walls been closing in, and she'd driven to the cliffs so she could stand and stare out across the ocean and get some sea air into her lungs?

What if it had been her driving, and someone had followed her and decided to push her?

But there was no evidence that Frances was dead. No body had been found.

The car had already been impounded for forensics to work on, and, since there was no sign of a body, the location hadn't remained cordoned off. A search had been done of the surrounding area by local officers, but nothing suspicious had been found.

Erica parked in the same car park where Frances's car had been found and then followed the footpath to the cliffs.

She didn't want to stand too close to the edge. The sense of acrophobia went through her, her legs feeling weak, her head going a little dizzy, her breath catching. The cliffs were over five hundred feet high and had views over the English Channel and Eastbourne. She couldn't picture Frances throwing herself from the edge. Erica didn't even want to stand near it.

She moved back to a safe distance, and the building anxiety faded away. It was beautiful around here. The grass had grown brittle and yellowed after the last few weeks of unseasonable sunshine, crispy underfoot.

Erica put her hands on her hips and lifted her face to the sun. She inhaled deeply. She still felt wrung through, and exhausted, and in pain, but she needed to focus on the case. It wouldn't help anyone for her to crawl into bed and pull the covers over her head, no matter how much she might want to. She'd suffered loss in her life, and she'd kept going, and that was what she needed to do now.

What else was around the area? Who might have seen the person driving Frances's car? It didn't look as though they'd stopped anywhere for food or fuel—perhaps if they had, she'd have been able to get a name from a credit card use or even an image of the person's face—but it seemed they'd come straight down the M20.

Erica thought of something. If someone drove down here and abandoned the car, how did they get back to London, if that's where they went? Even if they didn't go back to London, they still would have needed to leave this spot. Did they walk? Call an Uber? Or did someone else pick them up?

She took out her notebook and scribbled a note to remind her to get one of her team to call around all the local taxi offices and Uber drivers, see if anyone made a pickup from around this spot.

She stuffed her hands in her pockets and turned away from the cliffs. It was exposed here, and though it was still warm, the wind lifted her hair and whipped it around her face. More people walked by, some clearly tourists, stopping to take photographs of the view, while others were ramblers, in all their walking gear. She was aware of how out of place she was in her smart work clothes. She nodded and smiled at people as they passed, and most people returned the smile.

How had no one seen anything?

Erica walked slowly back to her car. She felt deflated. What had she been expecting?

She spotted a white snack van selling coffees and chips and bacon rolls parked a little way off the road.

She hesitated and then decided she could do with something to eat and drink. She ordered a coffee—black with sugar—and a bacon roll from the man serving through the hatch in the front of the van.

"Did you hear about someone jumping not far from here yesterday?" she asked conversationally while waiting for her order.

"Yeah, I did. Shame, but it's not exactly rare around here. There are some taxi drivers who refuse to take fares out to the cliffs, in particular Beachy Head, because they don't want to ever feel like they've driven someone to their death. You can sometimes see the chaplain driving up and down, keeping an eye out for anyone who looks like they're not just out for a bracing stroll."

He handed her the paper cup of coffee.

"What about you?" she asked. "Do you ever see anyone?"

He shrugged. "Only the customers."

"What about a car that was abandoned not far from here yesterday? I don't suppose you saw anything."

He paused for a moment. "Butter on your bap?"

"Umm, no thank you."

He slapped a couple of thick pieces of bacon into the roll and then handed it to her on a paper plate with a paper napkin. "Here you go, love. You know, thinking about it, I was here really early yesterday morning, and there was someone who caught my eye."

She perked up. "Who?"

"Tall fella who was walking at one hell of a march with his hood up. It was early—I like to catch all the dog walkers and morning hikers—so it wasn't even fully light yet." He paused and frowned. "Why are you asking?"

She reached into her pocket and took out her ID.

"Oh, in that case the coffee and bap are on the house, love."

"No, I'll pay."

"Won't take a penny. Call it a thank you for all the good work you do."

She suddenly found herself close to tears, her eyes welling. She cleared her throat and glanced away, pressing her lips in tight as she pulled herself together. She reached into her pocket and took out her notebook. "What else can you remember about the person?"

He blew out a breath. "Not much. I really didn't pay that much attention."

"They were definitely male, though?"

"Yeah I think so. They had a black hoodie on, but otherwise they seemed too well dressed to be out for a walk. I think they were wearing smart shoes, you know? Like not trainers or anything."

She remembered how one of Ian Grieve's neighbours had seen someone lurking around in a black hoodie. Had it been the same person?

"Were you able to see hair colour? Or any distinguishing features?"

"Nah, sorry, love. Wish I could be more help."

"And what time did you say this was?"

"Just getting light, so around six, I guess."

"And you hadn't seen them here before? Which direction were they headed?

He nodded farther down the coastal path. "That way, towards the pub. It wouldn't have been open at that time, though."

Maybe not, she thought, but it would have been a good spot to have a taxi or Uber driver, or even a friend, come and pick them up.

She took the food van owner's name and contact details, in case she needed to ask him any more questions, and then gave him her card, too.

"Thanks for the coffee and bap," she said. "And the information, too."

The description of the hoodie matched the blurry images they had from the person driving the car. Now, they had a few more details—tall, well-dressed, male. It didn't narrow it down much, but it helped to firm up her belief that Frances hadn't jumped from the imposing cliffs.

Chapter Forty-Two

S he got back to the office.

Right away, she could tell something had happened.

"Where have you been?" Shawn asked.

"Sorry, I—"

But he didn't let her finish. "Another body has been found. Just been called in. The victim's chest has been sliced, just like with the first two."

Her stomach dropped. "Shit." Immediately, her thoughts jumped to Frances Gilchrist. "Is it the missing author?"

"No, it's another man. He's been found in a garage lock-up on the outskirts of Stepney. Local residents complained of the smell. Looks like he's been there a while."

Three violent murders in the space of a week, and a missing author. What the hell was going on?

"Shit. Okay, let's go."

She hadn't even made it to her desk, so she just spun on her heels to head back to her car. Shawn grabbed his stuff and followed.

Erica drove.

The tension between her and Shawn was palpable.

He wouldn't even look at her, and it broke her heart. She didn't want what was happening between them to affect the rest of the team, but it seemed impossible to hide the friction between them. It was like the elastic that joined them together was stretched to breaking point.

Would it break now?

They arrived at the scene of the crime. The garages were located down a narrow lane around the back of a housing estate. The area was already busy with SOCO and uniformed police. Erica parked on the road, and they suited up and ducked beneath the outer cordon. She was grateful for the mask she could pull up over her mouth and nose to muffle the smell. In this warm weather, she was surprised no one had reported the body sooner.

The sergeant in charge of the scene came to meet them.

"What have we got?" Erica asked.

"Unidentified male, mid-forties, found by responding officers after one of the other renters of the garages complained about the smell. I'm going to warn you, it's not pretty."

The sergeant moved out of the way so they could get a better view.

Erica couldn't help herself. "Jesus Christ."

The naked man was tied to a chair. Huge folds of fat and flesh rolled over his wide thighs. Thick ankles, black with settled blood, had folds upon folds. Large breasts and meaty arms swamped his form. She couldn't even see his pubic area. That he was both huge and naked wasn't even the most shocking part.

The man's body was covered in cuts, as though someone had bled him to death. His pale skin was barely hidden beneath the crusts of dried blood that covered it. The spot beneath the chair was dark with what could have been an oil spill from a car previously kept in this position but was more likely to be blood that had seeped into the concrete over the days that he'd been in here.

"He's been dead a few days, at least," the sergeant said. "Post-mortem will tell us more."

Erica agreed. "At least a few days, if not longer."

Blowflies rose into the air around the corpse. Some smaller ones buzzed annoyingly around her head, and she batted them away.

"Look at this," the sergeant said. "I know it's hard to make out with all the other cuts, but there seems to be a few deeper cuts on his chest."

He was right.

One long, deep cut ran vertically up the victim's sternum. A second one below it, ran horizontal to the first. And a third, much smaller cut, was at an angle from the top of the first.

She put it together with the other letters that had been carved into the previous victim's chest.

This had become the killer's MO.

An 'N', an 'O' and a '1'.

"It's the number one," Erica said. "That's what the letters and numbers say. Number 1."

Shawn frowned in her direction. "What does that mean?"

"I'm not sure. Is it referring to the victims?"

"But there have been three," he said. "That doesn't make sense."

She stared at the bloodied body of the man in the chair. "This victim might have been killed first, which makes him number one?"

"Unless the murderer is referring to himself," the sergeant suggested.

Number one killer.

Crazily, Erica wondered if Frances Gilchrist had ever written a scene like this in one of her books.

"Or number one fan," she said.

Could this be who is responsible? Someone copying Frances's books as a way of proving what a huge fan they were? It seemed unlikely, and she didn't even know if the way this most recent victim had been murdered had been taken from one of Frances's books, but what if it had…?

Erica kept her thoughts to herself, for the moment. The sergeant didn't know the background to the other cases, and she wanted to check herself before going down that route. She could be completely wrong. She did plan to speak to someone who knew Frances Gilchrist's books from cover to cover, though, and find out if this had been one of the cases she'd written about.

She stepped back and checked outside. "No cameras, but that's not a surprise. Whoever is doing this is clever enough not to get themselves caught that easily. Until we get an approximate time of death from the pathologist, it's not going to be easy finding witnesses either."

He'd been dead several days, which made things harder. Time was not a murder detective's friend. It corroded evidence and faded witness's memories. The longer that went between a murder and the suspect being caught was linear to the chances of them solving the case.

The area where the body had been found consisted of a bank of five garages with a small parking area outside of them.

"Who do they belong to?" she asked the sergeant.

"Council owned. They rent them out to local residents, but this one's been standing empty for a while. Council said the roof's been leaking, which is why they hadn't rented out it. They just haven't got around to fixing it yet."

"Unused parking in London." She raised her eyebrows. "They must have people killing themselves for this." She winced at her use of language. "Sorry. Let's find out who rents these other garages. Maybe they saw or heard something."

From the amount of blood on the ground, it appeared as though the victim had been killed here. The way the blood remaining in his body had settled around his ankles and the wide expanse of his backside, like a black tidemark, also suggested that he hadn't been moved.

She thought about the position of the garages again. They were tucked away, down a narrow lane. Unless you knew they were there, a person wouldn't just come across them. Whoever used the garage knew both its location and that it was empty.

"Let's speak to whoever deals with the garages at the council, too," she said to Shawn. "Check their backgrounds. Who would have known the garage was empty? And who was renting it before it ended up empty? By the look of it, it took some time for this poor bastard to die. Someone knew they weren't going to be disturbed."

Chapter Forty-Three

It had taken awhile after Blaire had left for Frances to pull herself back together again. She'd been hysterical, crying herself into exhaustion. She didn't know how she was going to do this.

He'd taken the laptop away again. It needed charging, and she assumed he didn't trust her with the lead. Maybe he thought she'd use it as a weapon, or perhaps he thought she might use it to try and strangle herself, choosing death over trying to give him what he wanted.

It meant she was back in the dark. At first, she didn't even care, but then it started doing strange things to her mind. She kept imagining someone else in the room with her, or that she could hear noises, a humming or buzzing, but wasn't sure if it was from somewhere in the room or if her ears were playing tricks on her.

Though she didn't have any appetite, when she put her hand on the plastic wrapping of the sandwich he'd brought her, her stomach clenched. She didn't know how long it had been since she'd last eaten, but she figured it must be close to twenty-four hours now. The sandwich was basic—white bread with plastic cheese and ham slices—but it was better than nothing. She took one tentative bite, and her mouth flooded with saliva. She ate the rest with a ferocious hunger that took over, so it was as though she ate in a kind of trance, and, when she was finally licking those final crumbs from her fingers, she could barely recall actually eating it.

She felt better with something in her stomach, though. Stronger. She still didn't know how she was going to give Blaire what he wanted, but for now she just wanted to rest.

How badly would he hurt her?

At least he hadn't touched her like *that*. She doubted he would either. She'd always had her suspicions that Blaire was gay. Not that she cared in the slightest, or at least hadn't until now. She'd thought he was a good guy. A little intimidating, perhaps, but then she found most people intimidating. Now it was like he was a whole different person.

Her thoughts drifted into a doze.

Her head was filled with dreams. Strange things that didn't seem to have any connection or make sense. Birds with curved wings, flitting across a blue sky. What were they? Swallows? No, not swallows—their tails were wrong—these were swifts.

She jerked awake again. Swift. The detective she'd spoken to. DI Swift.

Had the detective believed her? Could it be possible DI Swift was still on her case? Maybe she hadn't been fooled by the car being left at Dover? Frances had told her that she'd believed someone might be stalking her.

Was hope a dangerous thing?

Chapter Forty-Four

Back in the office, Lewis Crowe lurked around Erica's desk, clearly wanting to speak to her about something.

"Can I help you, DC Crowe?" she asked.

He took a step closer. "I hope it's okay, but I was going over the photographs from Taylor Quigley's case file. I saw something in his room. I don't know if it's relevant or not, but I wanted to mention it."

"Mention it, please. Every detail is important."

"Do you see this ticket stub?" He pushed a printout onto her desk and pointed at an image that he'd blown up. "It's a coat ticket from one of the clubs in Soho."

"Okay, so we know Taylor went there. That's good. It's important that we're able to retrace his routes."

But Lewis shook his head. "No, you don't understand. It's a gay bar. I know because..." He tailed off, and understanding dawned.

"Aah, I see."

She didn't care if the new officer was gay or not. It made no difference to her. Did that mean Taylor had also been gay? It wasn't something his friends or family had mentioned, but perhaps Taylor simply hadn't come out yet. Maybe he'd still had his own doubts and visiting a bar like that had been his way of trying to figure things out in his head.

But what about the second victim? He'd been married for years. Some people, especially of the older generation, never came to terms with their sexuality. They used marriage and children to hide who they really were. Some of them even died with that secret. Could Ian Grieve have been one of them?

Could that be the thing connecting the victims? Was it what was connecting this third victim, too?

That wasn't a conversation she wanted to have with Ian Grieve's widow, but she also couldn't risk *not* having the conversation. There was a balance in it—being respectful of the victims and their families while still making sure they did their jobs. She didn't want to destroy the memory of someone they loved, but unfortunately, sometimes their investigations did reveal things about the departed that their loved one might have preferred not to know. There was a special kind of cruelty in it—discovering someone who was now dead had lied about who they were. It wasn't as though the person they'd left behind could ever get any closure or explanation. She wasn't saying that this was the case for Ian Grieve, but it was something she'd come across before.

If there was any possibility that this was the thing connecting them, it might give them a new lead. The murders could be hate crimes.

Though she'd have preferred to have brought up such a sensitive topic in person, she found Joyce Grieve's phone number and called her.

"I'm sorry to have to bring this up," Erica said to the older woman once she'd introduced who she was, "but what was the relationship like between you and your husband?"

"We were best friends, always had been."

Erica felt horrible even implying what she was about to. "We have reason to believe the first victim was homosexual.

We're trying to work out if there were any connection between him and your husband."

There was a pause, and then Joyce said, "You're asking if my husband was gay?"

"I'm sorry, I—"

"My husband was bisexual, Detective. It was something he was always open with me about. I accepted who he was without question. He chose me. He chose me our entire life. Was my husband attracted to men? Yes, I'm sure he was, just like I'm often attracted to other men, but that doesn't mean either he or I ever acted on those feelings? We were faithful to one another."

"Oh, right." Erica hadn't been expecting her to be quite so open and forthright about it. "Do you know a gay bar in Soho? Is there any chance you husband went there?"

"He had friends who were homosexual, so yes, it's possible he went there. He had his own social life. I didn't require an update of exactly where he went and when. It's called trust, Detective. I trusted him completely. He didn't deserve what happened to him."

"No," Erica said. "None of them did."

So that was the connection. Was someone stalking gay bars, picking victims from them? But why had they been killed in such a way?

"Thank you for being so honest with me, Mrs Grieve. I appreciate it. This might be what we need to catch the person who did this to your husband."

"You think it might be a hate crime?" the older woman asked.

"It's possible, yes. We couldn't understand what connected the two victims, but now we have a lead."

"I'm sorry, I should have told you sooner. I didn't know it was relevant. It was just a part of who my husband was that I didn't even think about."

"That's okay." Erica gave a small smile, though Joyce Grieve couldn't see it. "You've told us now, and you weren't to know."

"I hope you find the bastard who did this to Ian. He should spend the rest of his life behind bars."

"I agree with you one hundred percent, and I'll do whatever I can to make that happen."

She just hoped she was going to find the killer before he did this to someone else.

"Can I ask you one more thing, Mrs Grieve?"

"Of course."

"You said that Ian worked at the council before he retired five years ago. I don't suppose he had anything to do with renting out garages to local people."

There was a moment before she replied. "Not that I know of, but then I'm not sure I paid enough attention to what Ian was doing at work. I hate to admit it, but it was a little dull."

Erica gave a small laugh. "Of course. Not to worry."

"Why do you ask?" she enquired.

Everyone was going to hear soon enough. "There's been a third murder, Mrs Grieve. We believe it might be connected to your husband's case."

A sharp breath came down the line. "My God. The world is truly going to Hell."

Erica couldn't agree more.

Chapter Forty-Five

Erica addressed her team. "We have a lead thanks to DC Crowe."

Everyone turned to look at the younger man, who turned bright red.

"Let's check arrests for any links to hate crimes against gay men. My guess is that they haven't just started with killing these men. They'll most likely have some kind of history of violence against homosexual men. Will they have been arrested for it? I don't know yet, but it's possible. The killer might have been building up to this. I also want someone down at the club where Taylor visited, see if anyone remembers him, or if they have CCTV from the night he was there."

"What about the way the men have been killed, and the letters carved into their chests?" Hannah Rudd asked. "Are they linked to the hate crimes? What do they mean?"

Erica shook her head. "I wish I could tell you, but the number one must mean something. Keep digging."

She also remembered how she was going to get someone to follow up on her suspicions about the person who was seen at Dover. "Lewis, since you're on a roll, can you also check up on taxi and Uber drivers who might have got a call from near the pub at Beachy Head the morning Frances Gilchrist went missing?"

"Yes, boss."

She left them to it.

Truthfully, she felt like she could do with a nap. She was exhausted, and right now the only thing pushing her through was adrenaline. Maybe Shawn was right when he said she should have stayed home, but somehow she knew that would only have made her feel ten times worse. Here, at least she was useful. She had a purpose. She wouldn't be lying in bed, beating herself up for letting everyone down.

From across the office, Shawn got her attention.

"We've got an ID on the victim from the garages," he said. "His name is Oliver Swaine. He lives alone in a bedsit, which is why no one reported him missing. He doesn't have any kind of record. No driver's licence. Not married, and no kids that we're aware of."

"Who do we notify of his death? He must have a next of kin."

"Not that we've found yet."

Erica wondered if he had any connection with the gay scene. She doubted he was in any kind of relationship, or someone would have reported him missing before now.

"His neighbour called it in," Shawn continued. "They hadn't seen him for several days and were worried, especially as they said he never went anywhere normally and didn't seem to have any family or friends. They were concerned he might have had a heart attack or something and need help, but then their description matched the John Doe."

Erica got to her feet. "Let's go and speak to them."

For a moment, the room spun around her, and she steadied herself with her hand on the desk. If Shawn noticed he didn't say anything.

"I'll drive," he said instead.

Thirty minutes later, they arrived at the property and gained entry.

It was a depressing place. A single bed along one wall. A corner set up as a kitchen, which contained a small fridge, a kettle, and an air fryer. The room had a sink, but the bathroom was a shared one with the other bedsits in the building. Dirty clothes were piled everywhere. The carpet was threadbare, and the wallpaper peeled away from the walls in the corners.

"Look at these," Shawn said, picking up a packet of pills from the bedside table. *Cipramil.*

"Antidepressants," she said.

Shawn grimaced. "Poor bloke."

The neighbours who'd reported him missing turned out to be other people who lived in the bedsit, the same ones who shared the bathroom. They were both men—one younger, in his twenties, and the other in his fifties, who'd just got out of a broken marriage, where the wife had kept the house, as he seemed keen to inform them.

Shawn ran them through a number of questions about Oliver—when had been the last time they'd seen him, did he ever have anyone with him or visiting him, did they know if he had a job?

"Yes," the younger man said, "but it was something to do with stuff online, so he didn't have to go into an office or anything."

Shawn turned to Erica. "Any sign of a computer or phone?"

"No, and the place isn't exactly big. If they were in there, I think we'd have found them by now. Whoever took him must have taken them, too."

She was being snappy, and she forced herself to take a breath. She knew people would tell her to be gentle on herself, too, that she'd been through a trauma and was grieving, and probably shouldn't even be back at work yet, but she couldn't face staying home either.

Far worse things happened to people every day—she, of all people, should know that. Just look at this most recent development. The victim was in his forties and yet lived alone, in this shit-hole, with no friends or family to speak of. How tragic that his life ended in such a terrible way. He was never given a chance for things to get better.

Then she realised how judgemental she was being. Perhaps Oliver had been happy living here. He might have been a natural recluse who enjoyed living his life online. The antidepressants on the bedside table said otherwise, however.

"Who was he working for?" Shawn asked the young man.

"Lots of different people. He worked freelance creating online content. Short video clips for companies to use on social media."

Shawn addressed Erica. "If we get bank details, we might be able to narrow down who was paying him from there."

She nodded. "Good thinking."

Maybe the men were gay, and perhaps that was how their killer had made a connection with them, had got to know them even, but there were other connections, too. Other ways they might have caught the murderer's eye.

Chapter Forty-Six

Despite the lead they had, something was still worrying at the back of Erica's mind. Frances Gilchrist was still missing.

When they finished at Oliver Swaine's bedsit, she called Frances's agent, William Hart.

She wished Frances was around so she could ask her directly, though if this was a case of Frances being paranoid, perhaps it was best that she didn't feed the beast. It could all just be a wild flight of fancy, but putting those thoughts into Frances's head wouldn't help things.

"My name is DI Swift, and I'm investigating a case," she said.

"Frances's case?" His tone contained a level of urgency. "Is there any news on her whereabouts yet?"

"Not yet, I'm sorry. I actually wanted to speak to you about something else. How well do you know Frances Gilchrist's books?"

"Well enough. I always make sure I've read an upcoming book before it's published. I don't believe I could do a good job of selling or promoting it if I haven't."

"You're aware of her claims that two recent murders have been based on scenes from her books. What are your thoughts on that?"

He hesitated down the line. "I mean, it's got to be a coincidence, hasn't it?"

"This is going to sound like a strange question, but do you know of any of her novels that contain a man being killed by a hundred cuts? The victim might not be the same—in this case, it's a heavy, middle-aged white male—but he was found in a garage, tied to a chair."

Silence radiated down the line.

"Mr Hart?"

He cleared his throat. "Sorry. I just—"

He cut himself off again.

Adrenaline shot through her veins. "You recognise what I just told you, don't you?"

"Yes, I do. The way the man's been killed is from one of her books."

"I thought it might be. This can't just be a coincidence—"

He cut her off. "Except this book hasn't been published yet."

She wasn't sure she'd heard him correctly. "What?"

"It's called *Seize the Dead*, and it's not due for release for several months. We've been promoting the preorder, but no one has read it yet, at least no one outside of her inner circle."

"So someone she's close to?" Erica prompted.

"Or someone in the office. Editors and proofreaders will work on the same book. No one person can pick up all the typos."

"How many people would have read it?"

"I don't know exactly. Five maybe, in the publishing house anyway. But who knows who else she got to read it. She might have asked friends or family members to read it before she submitted it."

"Shit. Would her husband know who else she allows to read her books before publication?" Another thought occurred to her. "Does he?"

"I don't believe so. She's complained on a couple of occasions that Matt never reads her books."

Was that the truth, though? Or was it something he just said in order to cover his back? Maybe this was a husband-and-wife team, and they were in on it together. One huge publicity stunt.

The only thing that stopped her believing that theory was that she'd met both Frances and Matt Gilchrist. While she got the impression Matthew could be a bit of an arse at times, he'd seemed genuinely worried about his wife, and Frances had been one hundred percent genuine. Maybe it wouldn't be the first time that someone had fooled Erica, but for both of them to act so perfectly?

Could Frances have some kind of involvement? Was that why she'd vanished? Was she working with whoever had done this? Frances wasn't a big woman. Erica couldn't see how she'd have been able to overcome three men if she didn't have someone she was working with.

"Thank you, Mr Hart," she said, bringing her thoughts around to the phone call. "Would you be able to email me over a list of everyone who you can think of who might have read the book?"

"Yes, of course. I'll do it right away."

Or was she heading in completely the wrong direction? Would Frances have really come to see her if she was responsible for these deaths? Wouldn't it make more sense for Frances's suspicions to be true, and actually she did have a crazed fan out there who was not only stalking her, but who was bringing her fictional cases to life?

If that was true, then it could mean the author was in serious danger.

Chapter Forty-Seven

Locked in the dark, Frances had lost all track of time. How long had she been here for now? Days? It felt like a lifetime.

At some point, Blaire returned with the laptop.

"I deleted that pathetic excuse for a first chapter, Frances. I know you can do better. It was stilted and basic. I want to *feel* something when I read it. Make me feel it."

She was just grateful to have the laptop back. Where before it had been something to be feared, now she was thankful for the light. She normally wrote for escapism, but perhaps she needed to think of this differently. This wasn't escapism, because it was real life. No, she needed to treat it more like a confessional, like being in therapy, a way to purge herself of the terror inside her.

"I understand," she said, not daring to make eye contact with him.

Her scalp still throbbed from where he'd torn out her hair. What else would he do to her? He'd said he'd cut off her fingers, if it wasn't for his need for her to be able to use them, but what about other parts of her? What about her ears or toes? Were they fair game?

"Do you, Frances? Do you really?" His tone was low and menacing.

"Yes. My first attempts are often bad. It always takes me several rewrites before you see my work. I've been thinking about what I need to write all night. This time it'll be better."

She prayed she was making a promise she'd keep.

What if she tried again and again and again, and nothing she did was good enough for him? He was crazy, right? Perhaps he had an unattainable level of expectation.

There was no point in thinking such things. If she did, she might as well just give up now.

With a shake of his head, as though he'd already lost faith in her, he left.

She turned her attention back to the computer, but before doing that, she used the light from the screen to illuminate the pipes that she was chained to. There was no way she could get the handcuff off her ankle, not without breaking or dislocating a few bones, and probably removing a few layers of skin. But was there any way she could get the pipe off the wall?

She looked back to the laptop. Were there any parts that could be useful to her? Could she tear off a slither of metal and use it as a key to unlock the cuff? If she was in a film right now, she'd probably manage to do something clever like that, but she wasn't. Maybe there would be a part inside the laptop that would be of use to her, but that would mean destroying the machine. Her insides twisted at the prospect. Blaire would come back to a ruined laptop and no story. What would he do to her then? What was he capable of?

That wasn't the only reason she didn't want to destroy the laptop, though it was her main one.

She'd also come to feel like the laptop was the only connection she had with the real world. Though she was unable to connect to the internet, it still had that capacity. At a computer's keyboard was also where she spent most of her time, and though these were very different circumstances, it still felt a bit like being home.

Home.

A wave of grief, similar to how she'd felt when her parents had died, swept through her. What she'd give to be in her own house right now. To sit on her own sofa and lie in her own bed. She'd taken so many of the little things for granted.

She couldn't help her thoughts going to Matt. Was he sitting at home, grieving her death, believing that she'd willingly left him in the most final way possible?

Their marriage wasn't perfect—what marriages were?—but she'd never do that to him.

Her face was wet again, and she hadn't even realised she'd been crying.

Maybe she'd been thinking about this all wrong. She'd written the initial chapter from the victim's point of view, describing their pain and terror, but Blaire wanted this book to be his story. As much as she hated the thought of putting him in any kind of positive light, perhaps it would be better to write the first chapter from the killer's point of view.

She told herself she was just doing whatever it took to stay alive, that the book would never be published—she'd hit delete on the whole thing before she allowed him to show it to the world.

With a sigh, she pulled the laptop towards her and started again.

Chapter One...

Chapter Forty-Eight

There was no doubt left in Erica's mind that the disappearance of Frances Gilchrist was linked to the murders of the three men.

She called a briefing with her team and brought in the team from MisPer who were working on Frances's case. They needed to put their heads together on this now.

"We have a list of twelve potential people who might have had the chance to read Frances Gilchrist's book before publication. We need background checks run on each of them, and then we need to find out exactly where they were during the times of each of the murders, and where they were when Frances disappeared. We also need to consider her husband as a possible suspect."

Murmurs of surprise rippled across the room.

"I hope that we'll find Frances before it's too late," she said. "Now, does anyone have any updates for me?"

Jon Howard stuck up his hand and began to talk. "Boss, I was able to get some background on the garage. The person who used to rent it was an old boy called Gerald Rushbrook. He died four months ago. He was living in rented accommodation on the next street over, a bungalow, but he did own a property. Unfortunately, his health got too bad to be able to live there because of the stairs."

"He was still driving, though? He had the garage?"

"Yes, though probably longer than he should have been. He had a little automatic car towards the end."

"Did he leave any family behind?" she asked.

"Not many. From the digging I've done, they're currently fighting over the old boy's will. The house is in probate while it's sorted."

"Vultures picking over his bones," she said, a little judgmentally on her part. She thought about this for a moment. "Would any of the family have known about the garage being empty now?"

"Doubtful. They weren't close to him. They all either live abroad or several hundred miles away in different parts of the country. According to the neighbours, Gerald had someone who looked after him. A younger man. They said Gerald told them it was his nephew, but a few people raised some eyebrows at that."

Erica frowned. "They didn't think it was his nephew?"

"Apparently not. Gerald was known for being flamboyant in his younger days, and the neighbours thought the man who kept visiting him might have been more than just a friend, if you get what I mean."

Erica tapped her finger against her lips. "That would tie in with the other two victims. Perhaps if he'd also been going to gay bars—"

Jon spoke up again. "The problem is that Gerald *isn't* a victim. He died of natural causes. So, what's even Gerald's role in this, other than his old garage being used as the site of a murder months after his death?"

"You're right, but let's look into who this younger man is the neighbours were talking about." Erica thought for a moment. "The house is still in probate? Why is that? Who did he leave it to?"

"I'll do some more digging," Jon said. "See what I can find."

In the meantime, they had a lot of interviews to conduct. Was someone closely connected to Frances and her books really responsible? Possibly someone who also had a hatred of gay men?

Chapter Forty-Nine

Frances had fallen asleep again, several hours into typing.
It was amazing just how much she could get done with zero distractions. She had no internet to coax her away with promises of little dopamine hits from social media, no kitchen where she could distract herself with a cup of tea and a chocolate biscuit, no phone calls or bills that needed paying, or a house that was in desperate need of a clean.

She almost laughed to herself. Perhaps this was what she needed on a deadline—for someone to come to her house and chain her to a radiator until she got her work done.

Of course, it wasn't actually funny. People were dead, and she might be next. She actually felt kind of crazy about the whole thing. She had moments where she wondered if all this was real, or if she was stuck in some kind of nightmare. Or what if she had driven to Dover and thrown herself off the cliff, and this was her punishment? The eternal hell of her own imagination.

The thought of Blaire returning terrified her. Would the police have spoken to him by now? He was connected to her, after all. Surely they'd question him? How had he come across to them? The well-mannered, professional man he'd always seemed to her? They'd never suspect him of this. How could anyone even imagine he was capable of such a thing?

She was petrified of him coming back, but she knew it was going to happen.

Sure enough, another hour or so passed before the key turned in the door. Instinctively, she pressed herself back, trying to create space where there was none.

Blaire entered the room. He left the door behind him open, the light shafting into the room, as though he was in a spotlight on stage. It took her a minute for her eyes to grow used to the light.

She studied the space beyond him, trying to find some detail that might help her figure out where she was. The walls had old-fashioned textured wallpaper, but they looked as though they'd been painted over several times. The carpet was brown-and-orange patterned, as though it had come straight out of the eighties. It was a complete contrast to the room she was in—with its high-tech soundproofing—or the expensive laptop she was being forced to write on. If she could work that part out, maybe it would also help her escape. She didn't know how that would happen, but she wasn't just going to give up. Life was too important to her.

Was that why she'd been so afraid of losing it for all these years? The irony was that the more she'd feared becoming ill with something, the less she'd allowed herself to live. How much sleep had she lost lying awake, worrying? How many lunches had she cancelled because she'd believed she was dying of some kind of ailment or another? How many holidays had she backed out of because she'd worried about the country's healthcare system and whether they'd be able to treat her properly if she had a heart attack while she was travelling?

She'd made her world so small because of her fears.

"I hope you've done better this time, Frances," he said.

She didn't respond, but she thought: *So do I.*

He might be disappointed with her work, but she was the one who was going to be punished if he thought it was bad.

She didn't think it was bad, though. It had actually felt like an escape for a while there...losing herself in the story instead of dwelling on her current predicament. The hardest part had been knowing that what she was writing, was at least in parts, true.

Frances preferred fiction.

Not wanting him to get too close to her, she slid the laptop over to him. He picked it up and opened it, balancing the slim machine in one large hand while he read.

She felt sick waiting for his approval.

"This is good," Blaire said, nodding.

She exhaled a gasp of relief and sank into herself.

"Much better," he continued. "Of course, it will need my final touch as well, but you're definitely on the right track."

Because I described the killer as being strong and powerful and controlled, and knowing exactly what he was doing...

She kept her thoughts to herself. Pressed her lips together to keep them inside.

"I'm relieved to be honest, Frances. I'd thought you might cause me some problems."

Her body heated with shame. Was she bad for going along with what he wanted? Had she given in too easily? Maybe she should have fought him more.

But no, these were only words.

Words could be powerful things, but not if no one else got to read them. She was doing what was needed to survive.

"You're probably hungry," he said. "I debated on what I'd give you, depending on how well you did. If you'd displeased me again, you'd have been going hungry, but since you've clearly upped your game..." He turned and left the room briefly and returned with a brown paper bag and a takeout cup.

Right away, the odour of the coffee hit her nostrils. Her mouth watered, and her stomach groaned. The headache from the lack of caffeine she normally survived on, that had been thudding behind her eyes for hours now, finally threatened to fade.

He placed it on the floor, within her reach, and then stepped back.

She scurried forwards to retrieve the bag, the chain around her ankle yanking tight, and then grabbed it and retreated again.

She opened the bag to reveal a burger wrapped in greaseproof paper and a portion of fries. It wasn't the sort of food she'd normally eat—grease and arteries weren't a good combination—but she was so hungry she didn't care.

Snatching up a handful of fries, she shoved them into her mouth. They were almost cold, but they were greasy and salty, and possibly the best thing she'd ever tasted. Then she unwrapped the burger. It was also cold and a bit squashed and limp, but she crammed big mouthfuls in, barely chewing enough to swallow. If she choked, then maybe it would be a blessing. Like the fries, it was greasy and salty, but it also had the tang of ketchup and mustard.

Blaire watched her eat, an expression somewhere between amusement and disgust on his face. She didn't care how she looked to him or if he judged her on her table manners. It wasn't as though she even had a table. Whenever she'd been around him before, she'd always been so conscious of absolutely everything. She'd wanted to impress him, for him to respect her. She'd spent hours making sure she picked out the right outfit that said 'professional author' without appearing too businesslike. She'd been conscious of every word she spoke, how she sat, how many times she'd touched her face or fiddled with her clothes.

Now she wanted to smack herself for caring what this piece of shit had thought. Why had she ever thought he was a better person than her?

"I'm going to take the laptop away now," he said, "and work on the chapters you've done, and charge it up, too. Try to get some rest. I'll be back in a few hours, and then we can continue our story."

It wasn't as though she had much of a choice. Frances nodded but kept her gaze down, not daring to make eye contact with him.

She still didn't know how he thought he was going to get away with this. At some point, was she going to need to write her part of the story, how he'd locked her away in here and forced her to write?

How would he publish that without telling the world exactly what had happened to her?

Chapter Fifty

"I found a local taxi driver who picked up a man from outside of the pub on the morning that Frances was reported missing."

Erica glanced up at DC Crowe.

"That's excellent news," she said. "What could he tell you about him? Any chance he's got cameras in the car?"

"Unfortunately not, and the man paid with cash, which he said is unusual these days."

Maybe the person knew not to get an Uber, since everything was done via an app with all their details on it, and they'd paid in cash instead of a card for the same reason. This was someone who was trying to cover their own back.

"He was able to give a description, though. A tall man in his late forties to early fifties, and well dressed, though he wore a black hoodie over the top of his shirt. Said he was well spoken, too, though he didn't say much."

"Good work, that helps us narrow things down a little."

Could that be Frances's husband he was describing? It certainly sounded like him.

"Can you get some photographs over to the taxi driver? See if he can ID any of them? Make sure it's everyone who's already read Frances's latest book."

"Will do, boss."

A buzz of adrenaline went through her veins. They were narrowing in on him, she could feel it. He might have thought he was smarter than them, but the cage was closing around him. She just prayed they weren't too late for Frances.

From across the other side of the office, Jon Howard suddenly let out a yell. "I think I've got something."

Erica got to her feet. "What is it?"

"The will of Gerald Rushbrook. The one the family are fighting over. Looks like he left the majority of his estate, which wasn't anything huge, to someone outside of the family. My guess is that it's the same younger man the neighbours were talking about." Jon took a breath. "His name is Blaire Foster."

She knew that name.

Erica grabbed the list of names that she'd got from the publishing house. There it was. Blaire Foster worked as Frances's editor.

"I think we've got him," she called out to her team. "Get onto the publishing house; find out if Blaire Foster has been in today. What's his address? Is it local?" She directed that last question back to Jon.

Jon was already on his feet. "Yeah, he has a flat on the Isle of Dogs."

"Let's get a team round there, asap. We need to consider him dangerous. He might not only be our murderer, but he also might be the reason Frances Gilchrist is missing."

Chapter Fifty-One

An Armed Response Unit was positioned outside of the flat on the Isle of Dogs where Blaire Foster lived.

Erica prayed they weren't too late.

According to the publishing house, Blaire Foster hadn't been into work today either. His boss said he'd taken a couple of days' annual leave. Erica suspected she knew the exact reason why.

The road had been blocked off on either end, and nosey members of the public were gathering, trying to see what was going on. It was hitting rush hour in London—the busiest time—and people were obviously not happy about the road being closed off.

"Let's make sure we've got the rear of the property covered, too," Erica said. "I don't want any possibility of him doing a runner."

Police officers in protective gear led the way. They used a battering ram to take down the door and then flooded into the flat. Shouts of 'Police! Police,' burst from inside the building, followed by exclamations of 'clear.'

Erica and Shawn followed them in, only to be greeted by the officer who'd led the Armed Response Unit.

"There's no one here, Detective," he said with a slight Scottish burr.

"Shit. Are you sure?"

He shrugged. "The place isn't that big, and there aren't too many hiding places."

She turned back to Shawn. "Then where the hell is he? And where is Frances?"

"The house that's in probate," Shawn suggested. "Could he have taken her there? Would he have access to that? Someone would still need to maintain the property, turn off the water, and air it out occasionally to prevent it getting damp."

Erica nodded. "And keep a local author captive."

"Shit." Shawn rubbed his hand across his mouth. "What the hell is his motive? He's worked with her for years. Why do this to her now?"

"He's her number one fan," she said, referring to the letters he'd carved into his victim's chests. "Perhaps he decided he didn't want to share her writing with anyone else."

Sometimes it was impossible to fully understand why a person did what they did. A psychopath would justify and reason to themselves about why it was perfectly acceptable for them to do whatever terrible things they did. Something that would seem unbelievable to a rational mind was normal to them.

"Do you think she's still alive?" Shawn asked.

"I really hope so."

Chapter Fifty-Two

The door burst open, and Blaire hurried over to her.

He was normally so composed—except for when he'd read her bad writing—but now he seemed wild. His hair spiked up all over the place, and she could swear she'd seen his eyes rolling, like a horse that had been spooked.

"What's going on?" she asked, her heart in her throat.

He produced a key, which he tried to use on the cuff around her ankle. He fumbled it, and dropped it, and swore.

"Fuck."

"Blaire, you're scaring me. What's going on?"

"We need to get out of here. Someone is trying to ruin everything."

Did she dare hope?

The cuff dropped open, but she barely had time to react. Blaire caught her by the wrist and hauled her to her feet.

"Get up! Walk!"

But she hadn't been on her feet for at least forty-eight hours, she was sure, and it was as though her muscles had forgotten how to send messages to her brain. She couldn't seem to get her feet to move, and instead of remaining upright, she collapsed to the floor again.

"I said get up!"

His grip was so painful, she was sure there would be a ring of fingerprint-shaped bruises around her wrist, if she lived long enough for them to form.

"I'm sorry," she sobbed. "I'm trying."

Pins and needles burst like flames through her feet, and her ankles felt like dead pieces of wood, but she did her best to walk. He wasn't making it easy, though, so he ended up dragging her along. He yanked her out of the room and into the dingy hallway beyond. What was this place? It was like an old person's home. The bright daylight hurt her eyes, and they welled with even more tears, blurring her vision. Still, he dragged her, barely giving her a moment to pull herself together.

What had happened?

He'd taken the laptop with him the last time he'd left. Where was it now? Had someone found it?

The screech of cars pulling up outside snatched her attention.

Blaire drew to a halt. "Fuck."

Car doors slammed, and Frances's heart lifted with hope. But then Blaire leaned down and picked her up, slinging her over his shoulder as though she were no heavier than a bag of flour.

"We'll go the back way," he said.

He spun on his heels, and Frances remembered that she was no longer cuffed.

"No! Put me down." The feeling had returned to her feet, and she had her hands free now, too. She pounded on his back with her fists and did her best to swing out at his head. But gravity wasn't on her side. He was fearsomely strong—something she'd never have picked up on about him—and she felt like a child in his grip.

Blaire hurried through the house and reached the back door. It was locked, but the key was sticking out of the keyhole, and he had to release her with one hand to unlock it.

"Armed police!" a male voice shouted. "Hold it right there."

He was using her like a shield, protecting his own body with hers.

"Don't even think about it," he yelled. "You'll shoot her."

"Just do it!" she cried back.

She'd rather receive a bullet than risk Blaire getting away with her and locking her in another room to write his story.

A female voice reached her ears. "Frances," the woman said. "Just stay calm, Frances. This will all be okay."

Frances lifted her head enough to catch sight of the detective she'd spoken to—the one she'd dreamed about when she'd dreamed about the birds. Swift. DI Swift. She was wearing black protective body gear, but Frances recognised her instantly.

Blaire started walking across the back yard. She couldn't let him take her again. She just couldn't.

"Freeze!" the police yelled, but Blaire ignored them.

They wouldn't shoot him while there was a chance of hitting her.

With a cry of rage and terror, she swung the leg that had been all but dead only a minute ago, and somehow managed to drive her knee into his torso. Unprepared for the blow and with all his focus on the armed police, Blaire was taken by surprise. He let out an 'ouff' and half dropped her. She took the moment to shove herself away from him, tumbling to the ground, and a second later, a shot rang out.

Blair gave a yell of pain and fell to his knees.

The garden burst into a whirlwind of activity. Police surrounded them—some pushing Blaire to the ground facedown, while others helped her, picking her up and moving her away. She clutched to them in relief, a part of her unable to believe what had just happened. One moment she'd been chained in the dark, and now she was out in the sunlight again, with police officers asking her if she was okay.

Frances didn't think she'd ever take the daylight for granted again.

Chapter Fifty-Three

E rica sat opposite Blaire Foster in an interview room. He was cuffed to the table between them, much how he'd cuffed Frances to the radiator at Gerald Rushbrook's house. There was nothing he could say to plead his innocence—not only had they caught him in the process of trying to move Frances, they also had Frances's testimony. They had yet to finish the search of the Rushbrook property, but a phone had already been found which they believed to have belonged to Taylor Quigley.

The gunshot wound to his leg had barely been a graze. The doctors had patched him up and declared him fit to be questioned. Erica was glad about that. Blaire didn't deserve a moment's more care than he was entitled to.

She'd already run through the standard questions for the sake of the recording, and Blaire hadn't denied a thing.

"What was the relationship between you and Gerald Rushbrook?" she asked.

Blaire gave a small, sad smile. "I loved him, you know. It might seem hard to comprehend that it's possible to be in love with someone who was almost thirty years older than me, but I was. He came from a different generation, though. When he was growing up, people didn't come out. They didn't hold hands in public. He used to tell people I was his nephew, and I hated that he was ashamed of who we were." He shrugged. "But I loved him, and sometimes when you love someone, you make compromises. If him telling people that I was his nephew was what was needed to make it work, then I allowed that. And when he got sick, I nursed him until he died. Because that's what you do for someone you love."

Erica almost found herself feeling empathy for the man. How many other people would do that for someone, even after they denied their relationship in public?

Blaire sighed. "But then, after he was gone, it hit me just how little he'd left behind. We hadn't shared anything. Not a home. Not a family. He was just gone. That's when I started thinking about my own mortality and how I wanted to leave something of importance behind when I died. A legacy."

She sat up straighter. "And so you started killing people?"

"Words are what matter," he said. "They're the things that'll still be here, long after we're all gone. People talk about money or science, or others will say maths is the eternal language, but I don't believe that. It's words that truly make a difference."

"People didn't have to die."

"Oh, but they did. For the story, you see. Stories are so important. Take the Bible, for example. The stories inside that book happened thousands of years ago, but they're still being told. Maybe I'm mad. Maybe I'm crazed with grief. I don't know. I just did what felt right."

"You could have just written something," she suggested. "You didn't have to involve Frances Gilchrist."

He gave a cold laugh at that. "People who can, do, and I guess people who can't, edit. I did want them to be my own words, I really did, but I couldn't do it. I needed help, and I knew Frances was the right person. She never fought against me. Every time I made a suggestion, she went with it."

Poor Frances. If only she'd been a bit more of a diva about her work, she might not have caught Blaire's eye.

Erica paused the interview. She needed some more coffee. She was still drained from the last few days and what had happened, but she was looking forward to going home and finally getting some rest.

She left the interview room to find Shawn was there waiting for her.

"How did it go?" he asked.

"As well as can be expected. He'll be spending the rest of his life behind bars."

"And how are you?" he asked.

"As well as can be expected," she repeated. She pressed her lips together and then added, "I'm sorry for everything."

He nodded. "Yeah, me, too." He took a breath and then fixed his gaze to hers, dark brown to pale blue. "If you had to choose, Erica, what would it be? Having me at home or keeping me at my position at work."

Her heart clenched. "You can't expect me to answer that."

"Why not? It's a perfectly reasonable question, and the thing is, Erica, it wouldn't be one most people would struggle to answer. Most people would say they wanted their partner at home above all else."

"It's different with us. You know it is."

"Is it? Why?"

She shook her head. "I shouldn't need to answer that. You know why it's different. We help people. We save lives."

"We can still help people and save lives in different job roles." He closed his eyes and nodded. "It's okay. You made your choice. I guess we'll all have to live with that."

Chapter Fifty-Four

Several weeks had passed since Blaire Foster's arrest. Shawn had moved out and was now staying with his cousin. They still saw each other almost every day, but it was hard.

Erica had reached her car parked outside the station. She needed to pick Poppy up from Natasha's. She was doing her best to be there more for Poppy, since it was back to it just being the two of them again. She knew all of this had broken her daughter's heart as much as it had hers.

"DI Swift?"

Erica turned at the voice.

Frances Gilchrist stood behind her with a bunch of flowers—a pink and purple array of calla lilies and lisianthus—in her hands.

"Frances," Erica said in surprise. "How are you?"

Frances gave a tiny nod. "Doing better, thanks to you. I don't even want to think about what might have happened if you hadn't believed in me."

"And your husband" Erica said. "He believed in you, too. He knew you couldn't have done what your editor made out you'd done."

"I know. He's a keeper." She shoved the flowers in Erica's direction. "Sorry, these are for you. I know it's not much...considering..."

"They're lovely, thank you. You didn't need to, though."

She gave a small smile. "I did."

"How have things been?" Erica asked.

"Hard, at first, but I think they're getting better. The doctor gave me some medication for my anxiety, and though I didn't want to go on any pills, they are helping. I'm seeing a therapist, too, not only to talk through what happened, but also to talk about when I lost my mum and dad and how it's made me feel ever since."

"That's good," Erica said. "It's important to talk."

If only she could make Shawn see that. He'd shut off from her emotionally. He was trying to protect his heart, but he'd taken hers with him. He was still around for Poppy, and she appreciated that, but it didn't make things any easier.

"What about the books?" Erica asked. "You still writing?"

"Not at the moment. Every time I sat down at my laptop I was taken back to that room, you know? It triggered me. And then I thought about what I might write, and the thought of writing another crime and it inspiring someone else was just too much."

Erica offered her a reassuring smile. "You know that something like this is never going to happen again. Blaire won't be seeing the outside of a prison cell in his lifetime."

"Even so, I thought if I do ever get back to writing, I might try a different genre. Women's fiction, maybe. Something with a little less death and violence."

"I'm sure whatever you choose to do, you'll be a success at it. You're an excellent writer. I read the two books you gave me."

Frances blinked in surprise. "You did?"

"Yes, once the case was done and I had a little downtime. They were excellent. I might even go back and read the rest of the series."

"Thanks."

"Don't give up your calling," Erica said, thinking of everything she'd lost. "Sometimes it's all we have."

Loved what you've read? Don't miss out on book fourteen of the series, The Syndicate! Order now from Amazon!

. . . .

Get a free book when you sign up to M K Farrar's newsletter

mkfarrar.com

The gruesome discovery of the body of a middle-aged man launches a brand new investigation for DI Erica Swift and her team.
Don't miss out on book fourteen of this heart-racing, British detective series. Order now from Amazon!

Acknowledgements

D o *not* read these acknowledgments if you haven't yet read the book as it contains spoilers. I'm not sure why anyone would want to read the acknowledgments first, but I guarantee if I didn't put this warning in, someone would. So have you finished the book? Yes? Great. You may continue...

In *The Wordsmith*, I said several times that those who can't write, edit. I do not mean this in the slightest, and I would like to introduce you to two of my fabulous editors, who are also excellent authors.

First of all, if you're a lover of crime and gangland fiction, you won't want to miss out on Emmy Ellis. She's a prolific writer, and I genuinely have no idea how many books she has out. You can find all her books on Amazon on her author page[1].

Secondly, if you love cozy mysteries, make sure you check out my other editor/proofreader, Virginia K Bennett. She writes short, fun stories where a body is always discovered. You can also find her books on her Amazon author page[2].

I'd also like to thank my proofreaders, Tammy Payne, and Jacqueline Beard for always being that much needed final set of eyes.

And finally, thanks to you the reader, for following along with Erica and Shawn. I hope you'll keep reading!

Until next time!

---

1. https://www.amazon.co.uk/stores/Emmy-Ellis/author/B07HYPTTVY?

2. https://www.amazon.co.uk/stores/Virginia-K.-Bennett/author/ B0BTMWFYG9

MK Farrar

About the Author

• • • •

M K FARRAR HAS PENNED more than thirty novels of psychological noir and crime fiction. A British author, she lives in the countryside with her three children and a menagerie of rescue pets.

When she's not writing—which isn't often—she balances out all the murder with baking and binge-watching shows on Netflix.

You can find out more about M K and grab a free book via her website, https://mkfarrar.com

She can also be emailed at mk@mkfarrar.com. She loves to hear from readers!

Also by the Author

Law of Sandtown

The Scorched Girls

Under the Surface

One Final Shot

DI Erica Swift Thriller

The Eye Thief

The Silent One

The Artisan

The Child Catcher

The Body Dealer

The Mimic

The Gathering Man

The Only Witness

The Foundling

. . . .

Detective Ryan Chase Thriller

Kill Chase

Chase Down

Paper Chase

Chase the Dead

Silent Chase

. . . .

Crime After Crime

Watching Over Me

Down to Sleep

If I Should Die

• • • •

Standalone Psychological Thrillers

Some They Lie

On His Grave

21 Days

In the Woods

Printed in Great Britain
by Amazon